Anomaly
at
Fortune Lake

ISBN 978-1-927438-09-1
Printed in the United States

Powell River Books
Powell River BC, Canada

Book sales online at:
www.powellriverbooks.com
phone: 604-483-1704
email: wlutz@mtsac.edu

10 9 8 7 6 5 4 3 2 1

Anomaly
at
Fortune Lake

Wayne J. Lutz

2012
Powell River Books

Books by Wayne J. Lutz

Coastal British Columbia Stories
Up the Lake
Up the Main
Up the Winter Trail
Up the Strait
Up the Airway
Farther Up the Lake
Farther Up the Main
Farther Up the Strait
Cabin Number 5
Off the Grid

Science Fiction Titles
Echo of a Distant Planet
Inbound to Earth
Anomaly at Fortune lake
When Galaxies Collide
Across the Galactic Sea

This story is fictional, and the characters are not based on any real persons (except John and Cassiopeia). Fortune Lake possesses characteristics similar to Powell Lake in British Columbia, but all of the locations are fictional. The aliens are real.

Contents

Chapter 1

Night Lights

Before morning twilight reached the loft, Ashley awoke to a window full of stars. It was a moonless night, clear and unusually cold for May. For a few minutes, she stretched out under the thick quilt, just looking at the star-studded sky.

Justin slept on, oblivious to any rustling next to him. Still, she barely moved, nor did she turn on the light, gazing out the window with even more concentration. After a few minutes, she got up, grabbed the flashlight beside the bed, shuffled into her furry brown slippers, and made her way downstairs.

There was no need to be quiet on the squeaky staircase – Justin wouldn't even notice. But it was important to descend carefully. They lived a long way from anywhere, and Ashley had learned a long time ago to treat routine actions with an eye to personal caution. Living out here, she was more watchful of her step. They were a long way from civilization – even farther in the middle of the night.

Shining her light down on the last tread in the stairs, she stepped carefully onto the glossy gray floor, where the give of the plywood registered a familiar creak. She took a few steps across the carpeted living room; past the wood-burning stove that still glowed with a few embers. She stepped through the unlocked patio door (which couldn't be secured from the inside) and out onto the dark deck, starlight flickering off the water in front of her. It all looked the same tonight, yet oddly different.

Wearing only an oversized T-shirt, the impact of the cold gave her a pleasant jolt. But it was the stars that stopped her in her tracks. As usual on a clear night like this, the heavens gleamed brightly overhead. And the stellar reflections on the calm lake were stunning.

But unlike similar nights, she saw the stars with a new perspective. What Justin had shown her last evening was enough to get her attention, and it wasn't because of the beauty. Now looking up, she was filled with anxiety and discomfort.

Swinging her gaze to the north, the tall cliff blanked out most of the sky, all the way down to Polaris, the North Star. The Big Dipper, where they had seen the flickering light, was gone, swallowed in its descent behind the rock wall.

For the first time, she was afraid of the heavens. Ashley couldn't help but look to the north and wonder.

Chapter 2

On the lake

The next morning, over a cup of coffee at the picnic table, they talked it over again. As far as Ashley could tell, Justin seemed less concerned than she was about what they had seen the night before. Since he had the scientific mind in their small family, she took it as a good sign this shouldn't be as alarming as it seemed last night.

"Well, I've seen objects flicker in the telescope before, but never quite like that," summarized Justin. "The atmosphere can do strange things, especially when there are upper air winds and layers of temperature inversion. That might have been what caused the flickering, and the mind's eye can play a big part. I don't mean we're imagining things, but the brain can affect visual observations in weird ways."

"But we both saw the same thing, so I'd say that rules out imagination," replied Ashley.

"But Ash, I'm the one who asked you to come outside and see a weird star. So what I thought I saw could easily have influenced you."

"It was there," stated Ashley. "I'm sure of it. And that star was too bright for us to just dream it up."

"You're right, it was distinct. The galaxy in the background is listed as magnitude 8.4, and the flickering star seemed fairly bright compared to it. However, an object as diffuse as M82 has its light spread out a lot, so it's hard to judge. If I were to guess, I'd put the star at tenth magnitude or so. In my small telescope, it would've been difficult to see if it weren't for the flashing which got our attention."

Justin, an experienced amateur astronomer, had viewed M82 many times. In fact, it was on his favorites list for almost any clear night when it was above the horizon. Unfortunately, the tall cliff limited the horizon to the north, where the galaxy resides. The stationary North

Star poked in and out of tree branches, depending on the extent of the wind and the current position of their floating home.

Justin and Ashley lived in a float cabin on Fortune Lake, two hundred miles north of Vancouver. Their home was an all-season residence, while most of the dwellings on the lake were occupied only part-time. Although this was their full-time house, the off-the-grid environment made it seem appropriate to call their home a "cabin." After all, it was small by urban standards, and its design was rustic. "Cabin" or "house" made no difference – Justin and Ashley loved their floating home.

Thus, in their float cabin on Fortune Lake, Justin routinely viewed Messier 82, an irregular galaxy shaped like a cigar, during the spring, when the Big Dipper hung upside down above the northern cliffs. Last night, M81 and M82, side-by-side galaxies, led the Dipper in its descending arc towards the west while Justin pointed his Maksutov-Cassegrain telescope at them. In the low-power eyepiece, the two galaxies sat in the same frame of view, a rarity for the more than a hundred Messier objects.

In a small scope like Justin's, the spiral galaxy M81 looked like a faint oval. M82, on the other hand, demonstrated considerable detail, especially with a higher-powered eyepiece. At a magnification of more than one hundred, a jagged rift of darkness ripped across the center of the irregular galaxy, looking to Justin like a spacecraft, with the rift forming the windows of the ship. As usual, in his imaginative eye, it was fun to picture aliens waving to the people of earth as they rocketed past.

With M82 centered in the field of view, Justin allowed his eye to relax, a technique to achieve better visual detail. Using averted vision, he purposefully looked to the edge of the field, using the more sensitive extremities of his eye to improve the peripheral contrast. It was then that he caught a glimpse of a flickering star superimposed over the dark lane near the center the galaxy.

Twinkling images are common when viewing stars with the naked eye, caused by atmospheric currents. But when magnified by a telescope, glittering is usually based on routine defects in the eye or overstimulation of the retina from the brightness of the light. For a faint star in front of dim M82, twinkling wouldn't be expected. But this star definitely seemed to flicker, and at an unusual rate.

At first, Justin wasn't even sure he saw it. The star was suddenly gone, as if in a blind spot of his eye. Then it reappeared, but brighter than before, and stayed that way without flickering for about a minute. Then it disappeared again. This sequence was repeated over and over, but without a consistent pattern. Each time, the flashes seemed to vary in apparent magnitude – similar cycles, yet not quite the same each time.

After watching M82 for several minutes, Justin took a break from the eyepiece. Moving his head slowly side-to-side, he felt cartilage creaking in his neck. *Crunch, crunch* – it felt good to relax. Then it was back to the eyepiece for another look.

The sight that awaited him was just as he'd left it. The star fluctuated in brightness as he watched. Now gone, now back again. When he was ready for another break from the telescope, he realized what he was seeing was unlike anything he'd seen before. This needed a second opinion.

"Can you come out and take a look at something for me?" he asked, stepping inside the patio door.

Justin slid the door curtain open, having closed it when he went out to observe the sky, helping to block the cabin's interior light from his telescope. This sudden encounter with the well-lit living room would diminish his night vision, but he needed a break anyway. The twinkling star near M82 would get his wife's attention next, so he'd have some time to recover before turning to the eyepiece again. Meanwhile, Ashley would need to dark-adapt a bit before looking through the telescope.

"Sure. What you lookin' at?" asked Ashley, setting her e-reader down on her lap.

She wore a gray sweatshirt with a big purple *UW* on the front, and dark blue sweatpants, no shoes or socks.

"A galaxy called M82. But it's looking weird tonight, with a twinkling star that seems to be pulsing at irregular intervals. I've never seen anything quite like it before."

"A supernova!" exclaimed Ashley, as she slid into her fluffy slippers.

Ashley could talk the talk, but she wasn't an avid amateur astronomer like Justin. Once in a while she'd join her husband at the telescope when he invited her to see something special. But it wasn't a passion like it was for him.

"Don't I wish," replied Justin. "No supernova ever twinkled like this."

"Could be a first."

"Nah. Who wants to be that famous?"

So Ashley went outside with Justin, and stood on the deck looking out towards the sheltered waters. She allowed her eyes to adapt to the darkness for a few minutes while waiting for Justin to re-center M82 in the eyepiece. The Maksutov-Cassegrain on its electrically-driven mount would keep up with the galaxy, were it not for the slight movement of the float foundation. As the cabin swung in the breeze tonight, the image would move off-center with time, requiring minor adjustments to bring it back into view. Once the galaxy was centered in the eyepiece, he turned the telescope over to Ashley.

"Take a look, Ash. I think you'll see a star in front of this galaxy that seems to flicker in and out of view. It's pretty dim, so you may need to tap on the tube."

Justin had demonstrated the "scope rocking" technique to Ashley before, when trying to pick out cloud band details on Jupiter. She moved into position, adjusting the focus knob a fraction of a turn to compensate for the difference between her eye and Justin's. She didn't need to rock the scope, because she immediately saw what her husband had described, and it was an image that would stay with her forever.

Chapter 3

Maksutov-Cassegrain in the Kitchen

When Ashley and Justin met, there were no thoughts of living in a floating cabin or anywhere other than a big city. They were both city-folk in the true sense of the word. For Ashley it was Seattle, where she graduated in journalism from the University of Washington, and then found her first real job at a literary agency. Within two years, she struck out on her own, working from her Seattle condo as a freelance literary agent. That's when she met Justin, right out of the Air Force and employed by Boeing in the 787 flight test program. His job was secure and lucrative. Hers was unstable and generally unprofitable. But Ashley had her parents, a financial advantage that didn't become evident until years later.

Justin Cambridge was older than Ashley by three years, which seemed a lot when they first married, but now appeared inconsequential. While Justin's flying career progressed nicely, it wasn't his idea of contentment. If he could break away on his own, the farther from civilization the better, Justin would be delighted. An outdoors kind of guy stuck in a city, he kept his eyes and options open. But as long as Ashley stayed in her niche as a literary agent, it was unlikely he could take the leap. Once Ashley Martin became Ashley Cambridge, Justin's income from Boeing had to be enough to support both of them, with her literary fees little more than a supplement.

Still, they both worked hard and enjoyed their jobs more than most people. There certainly was nothing to regret, but Justin's dreams of living far from the city never languished. Ashley, for her part, was happy as they were, but was prepared to follow Justin to the middle of nowhere, if that's where life led them. It wasn't until she got there that she realized how well-suited she was for life off the grid.

At age twenty-seven, Ashley answered the door one day to greet a new client, a writer with his first novel already complete but no prospects for publication. His letter of proposal caught her eye, but the sample chapters of his manuscript were even more striking. When she welcomed him into her home office, she felt a flicker of discovery in her gut. It wasn't often that an agent found a destined-to-succeed writer, and this looked like her first big breakthrough after years of mediocrity in literary promotion. Both author and agent were in a position to recognize pending success and jointly enjoy the ride to the top.

Just as Ashley and the prospective author were putting the first paragraph of their promotional plan onto paper in the form of a rough contract, the doorbell rang. Excusing herself, she went to the door with a smile on her face, not sure who would be visiting this time of day. Nobody could permanently interrupt her sense of finally-I've-arrived. A quick trip to the door, and they would get on with their high-spirited plans.

But when Ashley answered the door, everything changed. Two local police officers were there to give her the news: her parents had been killed in an automobile accident. It happened that suddenly. They were gone.

* * * * *

Not only was the trauma personally difficult, Ashley was an only child. So she really had no one but Justin to share her grief and help her prepare her parents' old house for sale. Since the home was recently refinanced for another 20 years, it was a lot of grunt work for very little monetary return. But after sorting through her parents' things, an emotionally exhausting process, and finally selling the house in a buyer's market, at least it was over.

Still sporting twin pig-tails at age twenty-seven, Ashley dressed the part of a teen-age rock star, while acting as a literary agent. The dichotomy was pronounced, but the publishing industry was changing. Almost all of her work could be done from home, with only an occasional formal meeting. Her regular attire included jeans, sweatshirt, and a baseball cap with her pig-tails dangling out the back. Only the color of the shirt and its logo seemed to change from day to day. That was fine with Justin, who grew into adulthood in an olive-drab Air Force flight suit, followed by a blue Boeing jumpsuit. He felt more comfortable in baggy pants and a T-shirt, which was where he wanted to be in life, preferably living in a remote region of this country or another.

* * * * *

A full year after the death of Ashley's parents, she and Justin were watching *Antiques Road Shows* on PBS when they saw an end-of-program advertisement for a future episode: "If you have something to show us during our upcoming road show in Olympia, Washington, give us a call."

"Maybe we could go to the show," commented Justin. "It always looks like such fun on TV."

"But it'd be more fun if we had something to appraise," replied Ashley.

"We do – or you do, anyway. What about that set of jade vases and bowls from your mother's house?"

"I couldn't sell them. Mom loved them so much, although she didn't really know how far back in the family they went. Her mother gave them to her. And my great grandmother had them in the family, too. But who knows if they're worth anything?"

"So this is a chance to find out."

"I could've found out a long time ago," said Ashley. "But I never took the time to have them appraised."

Which was just like Ashley, really not interested in material things, nor taking the time to consider financial implications.

"The show in Olympia would be a fun way to do it," replied Justin.

So they dragged the cardboard box containing the jade items out of the closet where it'd been for the past year. The jade might be valuable, and Ashley's mom treasured it, but she and Justin had little interest in such things. Their life was a city condo full of modern technology and very little history. For some people that works, and for Justin and Ashley it worked fine.

* * * * *

"So here's a jade vase, along with a bowl that's inscribed rather roughly on the bottom," said the *Antiques Road Show* interviewer, cameras rolling now for over five minutes. "And then this beautifully carved swirl of foxes in exquisite jade. Do you have a feel for how much these may be worth?"

"Not really," replied Ashley, a bit nervous after all the questioning on-camera. "I know it's been in my family for years."

"Judging by the vintage of these pieces, not just years, but centuries. And what pieces they are. The most valuable is the carved foxes, but together these items would bring a minimum of..."

To Ashley, the suspense for television seemed overdrawn. *Just get it over with, please.*

"… one million, six hundred thousand. These are some of the finest pieces of jade we've ever seen on the *Road Shows*."

"Oh, my. Oh, my," Ashley gasped. It was all she could say. Her heart raced, and she wondered if this was real.

But it was. Sitting in the wings watching the filming, Justin's heart felt like it was dropping through his stomach. They were suddenly very rich.

And thus, without a lot of further consideration, they sold all of the pieces except for one of the jade bowls they decided to use as a candy dish. To some it would have seemed disrespectful to Ashley's mother and all of the relatives before her. But to Ashley and Justin, it represented a pragmatic approach to their chosen lifestyle as modern young realists. Her mother wouldn't have been disappointed, for she always wanted Ashley to have a life even better than hers.

With this sudden unexpected inheritance, there was no need for Justin to punch the time clock at Boeing any longer, at least for the time being. He did the math, and was realistic enough to recognize that becoming millionaires when both he and Ashley were so young wasn't the same as hitting it rich in old age. They couldn't just keep spending and expect the money to last for another fifty years. A million sounded like a lot, but it wasn't enough for them to run away from their jobs when Justin was 31 and Ashley only 28, unless their finances were managed effectively. With good investments, however, they might be able to turn their sudden inheritance into a lifetime of pleasure. Or at least they could give it a try until someday in another decade they had to return (temporarily, they hoped) to a life of ordinary work.

It didn't take long for Justin to wrap up his job and move forward in a completely new direction he liked to call "very early retirement." And if Ashley wanted to pursue a literary career, finally writing rather than promoting, she could do that in her own "semi-retirement" in the remotest of locations. Even in the middle of nowhere. Which is where they went.

* * * * *

Ending up at Fortune Lake was a bit of a fluke. While camping in Canada, they rented a small aluminum boat with a 15-horsepower outboard motor, intending to spend a night on the north end of the lake a long ways from town. They'd heard about the floating cabins on this lake, practical replicas of days-gone-by when logging and fishing were the only industries of choice. Float camps for loggers and fishermen gave way to a lifestyle that was based on self-reliance and a different sense of purpose. Float cabins were built here by the locals as getaway destinations, handed down from generation to generation. Few lived on this lake full time, but a person could, with the right determination. And that was the single-minded desire when Justin and Ashley fell in love with a float cabin sporting a hand-written "Fore Sale" sign near their camping spot at Third Narrows. The misspelling simply added to the feeling of good fortune.

By the next summer, they'd sold their condo in Seattle, and moved into a floating home that was smaller than a studio apartment, less than 600 square feet including the bedroom loft. To say it was a change of pace is to say the very least.

There was no electricity you didn't generate yourself from the sun, the wind, or a few thermoelectric amperes from the wood-burning stove. Fresh water, a critical component of off-the-grid living, came from a hand pump that tapped into the cold lake below their cabin. And in the small "great room" encompassing the living room, kitchen, and dining area, they spent their indoor time, interspersed with numerous hours outdoors, even in the winter.

It wouldn't be simple. To stay in Canada for more than 180 days each year required citizenship or at least permanent residency, and that had become more complicated in recent years. But they submitted their paperwork right away, expecting it to take at least two years to even get an answer. In the meantime they played the awkward game of going back and forth to the States more often than they liked. "Flag-poling" they called it – leave and then come back to start the clock again. Technically, it was legal. Practically, it was uncomfortable. That's where Ashley's semi-retired status as a writer proved helpful, for their clearest route to permanent residency was for one of them to claim "skilled worker" status, easier for a writer than a very-early-retired pilot. Still, they'd need their residency cards as soon as possible. Until then, discomfort would eclipse their short vacations across the border.

For Ashley, it was a time to write, without all the interruptions that seemed so daunting to a writing career– no television nor Internet, and an hour's trip by boat from Blue Ridge, the closest town. The lake was deep, over 1200 feet in several spots, one of the deepest in British Columbia. But because of its depth, it never froze, so their boat could carry them to and from home even during the coldest days of winter. Which was a good thing, for there were no roads.

As for Justin, he was finally outdoors more than he'd ever been before. There was fishing, hiking, and exploring off-road by all-terrain vehicle. And finally there was astronomy, a subject he'd loved since a teenager. But now, after years of light-polluted city skies, he had a modern telescope with a Go-To computer to locate and track deep-sky objects in the dark of Fortune Lake. Justin stored his new telescope in a spot with easy access to the outside deck. He had a Maksutov-Cassegrain in the kitchen.

◊ ◊ ◊ ◊ ◊ ◊

Chapter 4

Eddies and Sea Monsters

Fortune Lake had a history of mysteries. The tremendous depth led naturally to sagas of monsters of the deep, including repeated tales of the Fortune Lake USO (Unidentified Swimming Object). Sightings of the USO were published in decades-old editions of the local newspaper. A grainy photo of one purported specimen on a beach looked a lot like a decomposed whale. In that instance, a "Letter to the Editor" in the next edition, alleged the photo was taken two hundred miles away on the Strait of Georgia.

On the day of Justin's sighting of the M82 mystery star, he and Ashley had arrived at their cabin late in the afternoon after a week away. During spring, when Ashley's floating garden needed attention, it was rare to be gone so long, but there was a writing conference for her in Vancouver, and Justin went along to remind himself why he didn't miss big cities. Yet, they had enjoyed their downtown evenings together, and had stayed on for an extra few days.

When they got back to Blue Ridge, they drove to the grocery store for a few items, and then directly to the marina. For the next hour, their 24-foot Bayliner cruised north towards Third Narrows, where they finally slowed to enter the confined waters near home, so their boat's wake wouldn't reverberate against their breakwater of floating logs.

As they eased their way into the channel near their cabin, the water in front of them took on an unusual state. Normally, this section of the lake was considerably calmer than the lower reaches, due to protection by the sweeping cliffs that marked their U-shaped cove. Even when storms pounded the rest of the lake, the bay adjoining Third Narrows was relatively calm. So calm, in fact, the currents flowing gently in and out were noticeable from the cabin, pushing wood flotsam on invisible tides.

Of course, being fresh water, these weren't real tides, but the river tumbling into Fortune Lake at the north end pushed the water south at a considerable rate. Meanwhile, the gates of the dam at the south end opened and closed regularly, depending on the local sawmill's need for electricity. Together, the rush of water into the 30-mile-long lake at the north end (top), coupled with the plunge through the floodgates at the south end (bottom), brought tidal-like currents to Third Narrows.

Today was no exception. The hour-long ride north in the Bayliner had been through mostly choppy water. But now, finally home, calm water greeted them. Justin eased the boat around a few sticks floating in the sheltered bay, slowly motoring towards the cabin. This was their favorite part of the journey. Almost home, and traveling slow enough to absorb the supernatural surroundings.

"Look at that swirl," Ashley remarked as they approached mid-bay, making the final turn toward their float cabin.

She pointed to an area broiling with a whirlpool-like swirl, only a few hundred feet away. Not ominous, but certainly unusual for this lake. Ashley and Justin knew this section of water intimately, looking out on it nearly every day in recent years.

"Must be the USO," kidded Justin. "Either that or they just opened up the dam gates big-time."

"That damn dam," chided Ashley. "But I've never seen anything like this before. Maybe there's a deadhead lodged underwater, and the water's swirling over it."

"Could be a sunken stump, with the 'tide' pushing in."

Justin aimed the bow of the Bayliner directly at the swirling mass of water, and then turned left at the last minute, propelling the stern over the edge of the eddy. It wasn't a major vortex compared to those in narrow sea passages, but it was unlike anything they'd ever seen on this lake. The Bayliner swerved slightly on its own, pulled back towards the whirlpool by the swirling current. A small application of power was all that was needed to veer back out into calm water. Over their shoulders, Ashley and Justin watched the eddy recede behind them. As they motored farther away, it seemed to dissipate.

"It looks like it's disappearing," said Justin. "Let's go back."

He turned the Bayliner around and headed back towards the spot. Nothing remained of the whirlpool except a ring of small chunks of wood like those that accumulated in near-calm water. The outline of the spot was thus obvious, but the swirl was gone. Justin looked across at John's floating cabin across the bay from their own home. Mentally, he marked the spot of the whirlpool by noticing how the line of trees aligned with John's cabin. If the vortex occurred again, he'd remember the spot.

Once again, Justin turned the boat around, and they headed towards their cliff-side cabin.

Thus, on their first day back home, Justin and Ashley found an unusual whirlpool in their own backyard. And that night, a flickering star. They often referred to their home as "supernatural," but it had never been as true as this day in May.

Chapter 5

Verification

The next evening was just as clear as the night they first saw the star, but with absolutely no wind. Thus, the conditions for celestial observing were even better, with no breeze to swing the float. Wind was always a factor when looking through a telescope on a floating platform. The computerized Go-To feature of the 125-millimeter scope relied on solid ground below, and a moving foundation caused a stumbling block. Originally, Justin wasn't sure a telescope of this type would even work at a floating cabin, since high-power magnifications presented an unusual problem. When the float moved, the telescope moved, and an object centered in the eyepiece might slip outside the field of view completely. Similarly, automatic tracking of an object would pose complications as the foundation shifted.

But Justin went forward with his purchase of the telescope he long coveted. And its performance surprised him. Yes, there was drift in the eyepiece, but most clear nights were calm nights, so movement was minimized. When the image did stray towards the edge of the field, the law of averages came into play. Even if a deep-sky object exited the viewing area completely, it usually drifted back in a few minutes later. Since the floating cabin was tethered to the shore by thick steel cables combined with a "stiff leg" log that prevented their home from smashing against the cliff, movement in one direction resulted in a rebound in the opposite direction. So tracking of celestial objects somehow sorted itself out. Often, on a calm night, Justin would leave the telescope on a target, go into the cabin to warm up, and return to the deck to find the object nearly centered in the eyepiece.

Tonight, with no wind, would only improve the situation. Still, merely walking around could cause movement in the eyepiece, so

Justin treaded lightly on observing nights like this. Hydraulic shock pads under the legs of the tripod absorbed some of the movement, and a little care allowed at least an hour to pass without having to realign the scope.

As soon as the first stars appeared overhead, Justin went through the simple process of aligning the Maksutov-Cassegrain. First he lowered the telescope to horizontal, and swung it towards the north. Polaris provided a good reference for this, since it blazed near the edge of the big fir tree directly to the north. Depending on the position of the float on a particular evening, the North Star was usually visible on one side of a branch or the other. If not, a slight shift of the telescope's position on the float caused Polaris to pop into view.

Once oriented with true north, Justin used the Go-To function to drive the scope towards two alignment stars. Tonight he selected Regulus in the west and distinctly-orange Arcturus nearly overhead, centering each in turn in the eyepiece and punching the "Enter" key on the Astro-Controller. Alignment was quickly completed, and he was ready to observe anything he might call up in the built-in computer.

M82 was first, of course. Using a wide-field 26-millimeter eyepiece, he dialed up "Messier 82" in the Astro-Controller, and hit the Go-To button. The telescope automatically swung towards the north, slowing a few degrees to the left of the upside-down bowl of the Big Dipper. For about another 30 seconds, the drive motor continued slewing at a barely-perceptible pace towards the target, and then stopped with a beep to notify Justin that the targeting was complete.

A glance in the eyepiece showed M82 nearly centered. With a slight adjustment of the drive buttons and focus knob, the cigar-shaped nebula sprung into 3-D. This is what made live observing with a small telescope under ideal atmospheric conditions so inspirational. You could never approach the detailed views found in professional instruments, but live viewing, coupled with the 3-dimensional aspect in a quality eyepiece, was stunning.

There was no flickering star. Justin switched to a slightly higher magnification by selecting a 17-millimeter eyepiece. With the Muksutov-Cassegrain's 5-inch-diameter primary mirror and its long focal length (by design, the light reflects back-and forth within the relatively-short tube), this eyepiece provided a magnification power of 110, high enough to easily detect the galaxy's central rift. Spaceship!

But no blinking star. In fact, there were no stars at all in front of the galaxy.

"Nothing unusual about M82 tonight," said Justin, when he went inside to warm himself from the chill of the May evening.

"No supernova?" quipped Ashley, a childish pouting pose on her cute lips, although privately relieved that the unusual light was gone.

"No nothing," said Justin. "Just the spaceship."

Ashley gave Justin a quizzical look, wondering if she was supposed to laugh.

"Oh, I forgot to tell you. M82 is cigar-shaped, but it always looks like a spacecraft to me, just floating by with lights in the windows."

"Oh," replied Ashley, not quite understanding.

"I'll look again later, so I left the telescope tracking M82. I'll check after dessert."

"You already had dessert. So soon you forget."

"A little ice cream would be nice, preferably with strawberries on top."

"No thanks," said Ashley, meaning it would be up to Justin to fix his second dessert. "I'm happy just to know there's no supernova exploding all over the place and making a mess."

* * * * *

After ice cream and berries, Justin returned to the eyepiece. M82 was slightly off-center, but easily corrected by the tracking buttons. Objects this close to true north rotated on shorter arcs, and moved out of the eyepiece less often. After another half-hour inspection, it was clear that the flashing light was absent. Which might mean it was a celestial anomaly that had come and gone in a very short time. Or it could mean it was never there in the first place.

After putting away the telescope, Justin used one of his observing guides to learn more about M82. Without Internet access, he did things the old-fashioned way, which is the way he liked it. It wasn't that they couldn't have Internet off the grid, or television if they wanted it. Both technologies were readily available through satellites, although such Internet access was still a bit pricey. Mostly, however, it was a matter of choice. They desired to remain removed from these distractions. Similarly, only Ashley's cell phone worked here in Third Narrows, operating off a power-boost antenna. Justin's phone was out-of-range unless he used the boat to motor over to Secret Bay where he had line-of-sight to the nearest cell tower. Of course, they could solve this with a satellite phone, but they chose to live with limited telephone access. If it was important enough, the Internet, TV, and even telephones could wait until their next trip to town.

So research was limited to books, and their home had several shelves of research volumes, even an ancient five-volume encyclopedia. Consider it a trip back to the twentieth century. And this suited them fine, except in instances like this when Justin would have preferred immediate news on a specific subject. If there really was something new in (or in front of) M82, it would be available on the Internet. What Justin and Ashley saw last night might have hit the astronomical headlines, although not the public news channels on their radio. So Justin was dealing with antiquated information from his paperback observing guide.

Messier 82 was the first known instance of a starburst galaxy, five times as bright as our own Milky Way. Located 12 million light-years away, it blazed in the sky nearly as bright as our galaxy's twin, Andromeda, which was five times closer. Originally designated as an "irregular" galaxy, research in 2005 detected two symmetrical spiral arms and an on-edge orientation that explained the cigar-shaped structure. A complex network of dusty lanes added to the mystique, hiding nearly two hundred young massive clusters in the starburst core, a perfect example of stars in the making.

Like Fortune Lake, M82 had a history of mysteries. There was speculation that nearby M81 once plowed through (or near) the galaxy, triggering new star formation in its wake. When the space-based Chandra X-Ray Observatory discovered fluctuating emissions near M82's center, everything stepped up a notch. Astronomers postulated that these emissions coincide with the first-known intermediate-mass black hole, although M82 also hosts a more-typical supermassive black hole at its core. Supermassive black holes at the center of galaxies (including our own Milky Way) are well known, but intermediate-mass holes are not.

M82, nicknamed the "Cigar Galaxy," was the source of unusual observations by University of Manchester radio astronomers in 2010. An object similar to better-known "micro quasars" was detected, sitting very near the center of the galaxy. It has a perceived motion of four times the speed of light relative to the galactic core, which is, of course, impossible. Currently, no theory entirely fits the observed data.

The closeness of more-typical M81, a spiral galaxy, and M82 in the eyepiece of a small telescope isn't an illusion. M82 is close enough to its neighbor to be gravitationally affected in a big way. Tidal forces have deformed it, causing star formation to increase. Thus, the designation as a "starburst" galaxy.

One piece of data that particularly attracted Justin's attention (besides the fluctuating core emissions) was the reference to supernova activity. M82 is reported to experience supernova activity at an amazingly high rate – an estimated super-explosion every ten years, reportedly caused by the galaxy's unique bipolar outflow of energy.

As an astrophysics junky, Justin knew that any galaxy he might select for study has unique and unexplained features. That's what makes astronomy such an exciting field. But M82 seems to top them all on the uniqueness scale.

After doing his in-home library research, Justin tuned in the local AM radio station before going to bed. The weather forecast indicated the clear weather pattern would persist for one more day before the next storm rolled in. So a third night of observation might be possible, if the clouds held off long enough.

* * * * *

The next night was marginally acceptable. As the sun dropped towards the horizon, increasing high-altitude cirrus clouds moved in from the west. Conditions to the north, where M82 sat, remained acceptable for now.

As soon as twilight allowed, Justin set up the telescope, again using Regulus and Arcturus as alignment stars. Amateur astronomers are generally better at constellation identification than the pros, since they routinely sweep over bigger expanses of the sky. Regulus, in lower Leo, required a chart, even for Justin, but Arcturus was one of the easiest to find in the entire sky: "Arc to Arcturus," using the handle of the Big Dipper to sweep to the orange star.

With his telescope alignment complete, he used the Go-To function of the Astro-Controller to drive the telescope towards M82. The Maksutov-Cassegrain stopped right on target, requiring only minor corrections to center the image. The cigar-shaped galaxy was still faint in the field of view, with twilight not completely ended. While Justin waited, he switched to the 110-power eyepiece, now barely able to resolve the galaxy from the gray-black background. But as darkness progressed, the image began to step out from space, although drifting a bit due to the breeze associated with the incoming storm.

Before it was fully dark, Justin saw the blinking light, just like two nights ago. Tonight he timed the fluctuations. "On" for 32 seconds, "off" for almost a full minute, and then back "on" for 43 seconds. As his timing progressed, there was no apparent cycle except to say the fluctuations were short, less than a minute "on" and "off," and slightly different each time. The star seemed equally bright compared to its previous appearance, and nearly centered on the spaceship-shaped galaxy. Movement within the eyepiece due to the moving float was considerable, like it was two nights ago. And the star was less distinct when it was "on," probably due to the less transparent atmosphere tonight. Moisture in the air, although invisible to the naked eye, could make a big difference.

After only a few minutes of observation, Justin went back into the cabin to ask Ashley to come out onto the deck to confirm his observation. He found her sitting on the old-fashioned coach with its upholstered cover of gaudy yellow flowers. Ashley's legs were tucked up under her, absorbed in an e-book. Her thin 5-foot-4-inch frame was like that of a little girl. But if you looked close, Ashley had healthy biceps and strong legs for a woman her size. No one ever accused her of looking wimpy. In fact, her college nickname was "Olive Oil," not too far off the mark when you noticed her almost skinny athletic build and her small breasts. She now wore her hair in a tight pony-tail, rather than the even-more girlish twin pig-tails of days gone by.

Ashley set her e-reader aside, and laced up her maroon high-top sneakers. Then she pulled a gray *Canada*-logo sweatshirt over her purple *Go Dawgs!* T-shirt. The neck of the sweatshirt momentarily caught on her reddish-brown pony-tail. She pulled her hair free, tugged at a blue hairband to slide it back into place, and then stood and walked to the door. A few minutes later, she was gazing into the eyepiece.

"Yes, it's there again," said Ashley, within seconds after putting her eye to the lens. "But I wish it wasn't."

"Don't be so pessimistic, Ash. Something 12 million light-years away can't do us any harm. Maybe it can eat our children, if we ever have any, but only if they live for millions of years."

"It's just that it all seems so coincidental," replied Ashley. "First the USO, now this."

Chapter 6

IAU

The International Astronomical Union is the universal reporting agency for verification of new astronomical discoveries. Nearly every day, a new celestial object is discovered, ranging from small asteroids to comets to extrasolar planets. Space-based telescopes had increased the number of reports to the point where the process is fairly automated. An email sent by anyone to the Central Bureau for Astronomical Telegrams at Harvard University starts the process. Yes, "telegrams," a throwback term reminding astronomers of the good ol' days when new discoveries came monthly rather than hourly.

But that's only if you have access to email, which for Justin means a trip to town. And if this is really a new object, it has undoubtedly already been reported. Amateur telescopes around the world routinely point towards M82, and Justin had already proved that even a small scope could detect the fluctuating object. Any observer, not only professionals, who pointed their telescope on the galaxy recently would have noticed the fluctuating object. Thus, the IAU undoubtedly already logged it. So was it really worth a trip to town?

The incoming storm posed an extra complication. Travel on this lake in any season was possible, but no boat was big enough to handle the most severe storms. This blow looked like it would be fairly minor, but weather forecasts in the region were often inaccurate, thwarted by the abrupt contrast of the lake and adjacent mountains. Expected clear days could turn into cumulonimbus clouds that poured rain, and stormy conditions routinely varied over the 25-mile span from Third Narrows to Blue Ridge.

"If the lake is okay in the morning, let's go to town," said Justin. "M82 is probably already in the astronomical headlines, but I'd like to make sure."

"Okay, we could use a few groceries anyway, and I can check on my Amazon numbers," replied Ashley.

If Justin was an astrophysics junky, Ashley was just as fanatic regarding book publishing. These days, that meant keeping track of her e-book sales and Internet settings on Amazon and similar online bookstores. She wasn't making a killing, but the sales from her new book about British Columbia history were pretty good. When she had access to the Internet, she used the time to tweak her book prices and category assignments. She'd learned that regular changes to such parameters helped the volume of her sales.

Lots of people these days shopped online for e-books, and you never knew where they might try to find yours. Besides, the extra income helped a lot, preventing the slow depletion of their investments, as was necessary to cover the routine costs of living off the grid. Their lifestyle was simple, but they didn't skimp on anything. Justin's Wall Street holdings were keeping the keel pretty even, but every little bit helped.

* * * * *

The purported storm was less than expected. As Ashley and Justin slept that night, occasional light rain pattered on the tin roof. In their bedroom loft, the drops were only a few feet overhead. As usual, the rain produced a mesmerizing effect that was almost hypnotic. Add in the slow swing of the float in the wind, and it was like a gentle lullaby.

The following morning dawned with drizzle, but little wind. Since travel on the lake was dependent on the waves rather than precipitation (even snow), conditions were good for a trip to town. Ashley prepared the cabin for departure, which didn't require much work. She emptied the garbage cans, putting the small bags inside a larger plastic trash bag, and carried it to the boat. She went back inside the cabin to close the venetian blinds and pull the curtains closed, and then grabbed her backpack and computer bag. She stepped back out onto the deck, locking the door behind her. They always left with the cabin secure, in case weather contingencies kept them in town longer than expected.

Meanwhile, Justin took care of the outside of the cabin, flipping off the electrical master switch so the solar panels would be able to concentrate on recharging the cabin batteries while they were gone. The propane would remain on for the refrigerator, and the tin boat could stay in the water, but he tested its bilge pump to make sure the float switch was functioning.

He hopped aboard the Bayliner, turning on the blower while he donned his red life vest, stowed their backpacks and computer bags, and then started the engine. On the deck, Ashley put on her bright yellow life vest, removed the lines, and stepped aboard the aft deck, intentionally pushing off with her foot so the stern eased outward from the dock.

Justin shifted in reverse to pull the bow clear, and then back into forward to motor towards the breakwater entrance. Then he angled the boat towards the spot where they had seen the swirling water on their arrival three days earlier. They had been watching this area from the deck of their cabin, but no further current was noticeable. However, since the area was about 200 feet from their float, any whirlpool action could be missed easily, except in perfectly calm conditions. This morning they slowly approached the spot Justin had marked mentally with reference to the line of trees near John's float cabin.

"It looks a little roiled, don't you think?" asked Ashley.

"Yes, there's still some swirling, but not nearly as dramatic as the other day. Look over there," said Justin, nodding his head towards a spot only about 20 feet in front of them.

"Maybe it's just started moving again," noted Ashley. "Otherwise, I think we'd have been able to see it from the cabin."

"Maybe."

This time the water was less roiled, and Justin felt comfortable cutting directly across the center section. The Bayliner barely reacted, drifting slightly to the side as it crossed. Compared to the whirlpool-like disturbance three days ago, this was a current that could easily be missed unless you were looking for it.

Behind the boat, they heard the mournful call of a loon, and they both turned around. To Ashley, the haunting cry always seemed to spell distress, but often it would occur when an inseparable pair cruised the surface of the lake only a few feet apart, as was the case today. The standard two-ship formation was travelling in-trail when the first loon began flapping it's wings, followed almost immediately by the second.

Loons take a lot of runway to get airborne. Some sources say they can't muster a takeoff without at least a little headwind. Their takeoff involves frantic flapping of their wings close to the water's surface. As they accelerate, they drag their landing gear as they skip and slap across the water. Their wingtips seem to touch the surface for the first fifty feet. And so it was today, until finally they were both airborne, skimming low over the water towards John's cabin. They quickly passed over a calm spot where there wasn't a ripple, their reflection making it look like a close formation of four. Ashley and Justin stared as they always did when things like this happened – in awe of the beauty of Fortune Lake.

When the loons finally climbed up and over the trees behind John's cabin and out of sight, Justin returned to the helm. He aimed their boat at Third Narrows, and pushed the throttle forward. The Bayliner stepped efficiently up on plane, and they were on their way.

The hour-long trip was uneventful, and they arrived at Blue Ridge Marina under cloudy skies with no rain and calm conditions. Justin pulled into their assigned parking spot on one of the inner fingers, kicking the Bayliner's ass around with a full turn of the wheel and a shot of reverse power. The boat came to a gentle stop at the dock.

From the marina, they used Ashley's truck to travel to their favorite Internet spot, the lobby of the local hotel. As usual, both of them had a lot of email waiting for them. After sorting it out, Ashley logged onto Amazon, and Justin called up the latest newsletter from *Sky and Telescope*, half-expecting to find something about M82. The weekly astronomy bulletin had been published the previous day, with no mention of the new object. Just to be sure, Justin checked his email trashcan for the previous issue, although he read each bulletin religiously and was sure he hadn't seen anything about the galaxy. As expected, the previous week's issue didn't mention M82.

So here was a mystery bigger than the galaxy itself. How could he be the only astronomer, amateur or professional, to have seen the flickering light? It was well within the resolution limits of all but the smallest of telescopes. Yet there was no news on the Internet. Not accepting the results, Justin googled "M82 news," and several hits came up on the first page. All of it was older than the current year.

Then, just in case – and what could it hurt? – he googled "reporting new astronomical objects," which led him promptly to the IAU Central Bureau of Astronomical Telegrams and an email link to the Harvard University address used for new reports. Without hesitating further, he wrote up his findings in a general paragraph that couldn't be misinterpreted. He explained the date and time of his observation, details regarding the size and eyepiece criteria for his Maksutov-Cassegrain telescope, and concluded with: "I call this to your attention in hopes of a verification for this observation by a professional source."

Verification of his observation by an independent observer would be essential to receive credit for a new discovery. Since Justin knew no one else in astronomy, he hoped the IAU would assign someone to the task. But they would do so only if he could convince them his discovery was both unique and valid. It was the valid part that troubled him. Wouldn't the IAU wonder why no one else had reported such an unusual circumstance? Observing schedules on a professional telescope were organized by observational priorities and commitments to astronomers who applied for instrument time far in advance. Breaking that routine would require something that seemed very important.

After sending the email, Justin felt a sense of relief. If he'd really seen something new, at least it was properly reported. All he could do now was wait.

* * * * *

After completing their in-town chores, Justin and Ashley headed back up the lake. This time Ashley drove, and Justin kicked back on the aft deck, watching their wake spread out behind them. It had turned into a beautiful spring day, the frontal system now past and the air behind it cooler. As the boat skimmed over rippled water, speeding north at 25 miles per hour, the clearing blue sky was patched with towering cumulonimbus clouds.

At Third Narrows, Ashley pulled back on the throttle, and drove slowly towards their floating home. All looked normal, including the spot where they again looked for the swirl. There was no sign of it.

The only interruptions to their complete serenity had been M82 and the twisting vortex of water. For now, both seemed put to rest, and their tranquil home on Fortune Lake welcomed them back.

◊ ◊ ◊ ◊ ◊ ◊

Chapter 7

Confirmation

After returning from town, Ashley fixed a big dinner, consisting of food they purchased in Blue Ridge that day: salmon with asparagus, and strawberry-rhubarb pie for dessert. Clouds moved in again late in the day, so the telescope remained in the kitchen, where it proudly stood next to their fishing poles and kayak paddles. Their small home was organized for functionality rather than appearance.

That evening, while Ashley used her laptop to work on her latest e-book, Justin read the newspaper from town and a few magazines he'd been hoarding for a quiet evening. As he read the latest issue of *Maclean's*, a Canadian publication similar to *Newsweek*, he couldn't help but notice how unimportant the stories seemed when compared to the discovery of a fluctuating star as far away as M82. And he wondered how soon he'd hear back from the International Astronomical Union. He figured there should be a reply within a few days. Either that, or he'd never hear from them at all.

"I must admit I keep thinking about my report to the IAU," he commented to Ashley.

"So maybe you're gonna' be famous, after all. Or maybe not," she kidded.

"It's just awesome thinking this might be important enough to have them point a professional telescope at M82," said Justin. "But how does the IAU decide when to do that?"

"Don't know. But it seems to me it warrants attention of some sort. How do all of those amateur astronomers who hunt comets get their observations confirmed?"

"In their case, there's a whole group of comet hunters who support each other. One guy makes the initial discovery, and another two or three join in to confirm the find. The IAU doesn't have to do anything but handle the message traffic. And the first fellow to report the comet gets it named after him."

"Or her," corrected Ashley.

"Sure, especially for comets. There are quite a few women in the field, but I'm not sure how stars like we saw are confirmed. There aren't a lot of people out there looking for celestial objects that flicker on and off. So maybe it will take a big observatory to confirm such a discovery. If it is a discovery, that is."

"Well, what else could it be?" asked Ashley. "We saw it, and you know it's something very unusual. So why wouldn't pro astronomers jump at the chance to confirm something so important?"

"But, Ash, it's a questionable object, and it's only important if it's real," replied Justin. "I'm still not sure it's a valid discovery. The most likely explanation of all is that we saw a visual illusion, which makes me feel pretty foolish."

"But I saw it, too."

"I still say you could have been influenced by what I told you was there. That's different from what was really there."

"There, where?" joked Ashley.

When Ashley kidded like this, her almost-round face revealed pretty lines that accented her overall girlish look. Justin loved it.

"Stop it! I'm serious about this, but I'm not sure I should be."

"So I suppose you should go back to town pretty soon to see what they say," said Ashley.

"If they say anything at all. But yes, I'd like to check my email within a few days. They'll probably reply, even if it's only: 'Tough luck – you lose.' Maybe I'll even go back to town tomorrow or the next day."

"Sure. Go tomorrow. So much for living off the grid."

* * * * *

When Justin checked his email at the hotel lobby in Blue Ridge, there was a message waiting from Harvard University, transmitted only a few hours earlier. It was a professional-sounding reply:

"We hope to convince the current University of Michigan observing team at Mauna Kea, Hawaii, to use a segment of their allotted observing time on the 8-meter telescope to confirm your report regarding the fluctuating light source near M82. If they concur with our request, that observation will be conducted within the next two days, dependent upon sky conditions."

The 8-meter telescope! This was one of the world's largest instruments, with tremendous light-gathering power. Justin pulled a pocket calculator out of his backpack, and ran a quick computation, converting meters to feet, and then to inches. Then he computed the area of the 8-meter mirror in square inches, and compared it to the area of his 5-inch Maksutov-Cassegrain at home in his kitchen. The big telescope on top of Mauna Kea had 3681 times the light bucket potential of his amateur scope. If it couldn't find the fluctuating star, something was drastically wrong.

But what was the punishment for wasting observing time on a professional telescope when it involved a hoax. Certainly it had happened before. Were the IAU police poised to make an arrest, and would it involve prison time?

Of course not. Stop thinking silly thoughts.

But when Justin left the hotel, his thoughts were still solidly fixed on the attention his email had received. If it turned out to be an observing error on his part, he'd feel terrible.

Back at the cabin that afternoon, he explained to Ashley how the 8-meter Hawaiian telescope might be looking for the object they saw in M82 as early as tonight.

"Mighty hot!" commented Ashley. "Which is the way all those Blue Ridge girls will think of you when you're famous. I'll never be able to get a date with you after that."

She scrunched her cute lips in her pouty pose, which always drove Justin crazy.

"Don't joke around like that," said Justin. "I'm gonna' be pretty embarrassed if this turns out to be absolutely nothing. So don't let any of our friends know anything about this, please."

"Sure. Like who? Maybe Jess when he comes up to his cabin about once a month. Who would you like me not to tell?"

"You know what I mean," replied Justin. "Don't even mention it to my parents if they phone, or anyone else in town."

"When you live way out here, you don't need to worry much about that."

* * * * *

Shortly after 8 am the next morning, before they were even out of bed, Ashley's phone rang. Hurrying downstairs in order to get the call before it went to voicemail was nearly impossible, so they didn't even try. Instead, they waited until the phone stopped ringing. Then Ashley got out of bed and went downstairs to retrieve the voicemail, if there was any.

In his email to the IAU, Justin left Ashley's phone number, since it worked here at the cabin. He yelled down to Ashley as she reached for her phone: "Could be them!"

"I'm dialing my voicemail now," reported Ashley.

Justin came down the stairs from the loft, waiting for her to tell him what she found.

"It's about your report," said Ashley, handing the phone to him. "Hit 4 so you can hear it."

The news wasn't good. The IAU had convinced the University of Michigan team to waste their time on a hoax, or what the Harvard official politely referred to as "your alleged finding." The astronomers at Mauna Kea found nothing unusual in the area of M82. The official completed his voicemail message by noting: "We request that you not refer any additional observations related to your original report to this agency. We appreciate your continued support of the IAU."

Very polite. Very awkward. Justin felt like he wanted to crawl into a hole and die. Or at least refrain from lugging the Maksutov-Cassegrain out of the kitchen for a long time.

* * * * *

After that memorable phone call, things began to get back to normal at Third Narrows. Ashley and Justin made a distinct effort to enjoy the great outdoors and their cabin on the lake. They let their lives return to simpler things, like spring cleaning and preparing their cabin for a visit from Justin's parents. Ashley spent a lot of time in her floating garden.

Justin rode his quad up into the mountains, where he tried to forget about his erroneous report to the IAU. He spent a lot of time as high up as possible. Similar to flying with Boeing or the Air Force, he seemed to think best when looking down on the world.

Ashley and Justin didn't talk about astronomical objects any more, but they still pondered the mystery of the USO's whirlpool. It was the kind of thing lake residents might dwell on and even enjoy investigating, so they checked the area where they'd seen the swirls whenever they went out in their boat. The whirlpool didn't reappear, and within a few days they stopped talking about it, too.

The weather remained cloudy and cool for several days, so Justin wasn't tempted to use his telescope, nor would he have wanted to look at M82 so soon after the phone call from Harvard. But after nearly a week away from his telescope, the afternoon skies cleared, and conditions were excellent for observing.

Shortly after sunset, without saying anything to Ashley who was working in her garden, he carried the Maksutov-Cassegrain out onto the deck, and set it into position on the corner of the float that gave him best access to the full sky. From her floating garden, Ashley looked across at Justin, caught his eye briefly, and then looked away as if disinterested. But he knew she wasn't.

That night, with a slight breeze to complicate his observing routine, Justin aligned the telescope on Regulus and Arcturus, and then pointed it at M82. The Big Dipper was still upside down in the northern sky, but was making its way towards the horizon as it descended while rotating westward. Even since his last night of observing, the difference was noticeable. Spring twilight was later now, and the Dipper was lower in the sky. A month from now, in mid-June, the constellation would be hidden behind the high cliff before twilight ended, and M82 would be gone. So another chance to see the fluctuating "hoax" wouldn't last long.

With the pending seasonal demise of M82 as his excuse, Justin focused on the galaxy. But he was determined not to take it seriously this time. Even if he saw the flickering star, he'd just enjoy it, and consider it a free but mysterious celestial light show.

Almost as soon as M82 appeared in the eyepiece, he saw it – "on" for about half a minute, and then "off." The event repeated itself over and over again at almost equal intervals. It was orderly, but not quite the same each time. "On," then "off," but with a pattern that changed each cycle.

Why was it so clearly visible to him, but not detected by a much larger telescope in Hawaii? And why was it here some nights, but not others? To heck with the IAU! – this was Justin's personal mystery to solve. He felt like Galileo, establishing his own scientific method as he went along. No one else might believe him, just as they'd paid little attention to the famous observer of the skies in the 1600's, but he would figure it out himself.

Which is the way you did things when you lived off the grid.

Chapter 8

Pillar of Power

"We could spend tonight at the Head," said Justin.

"That's always fun," replied Ashley. "I'll pack dinner, if you'll get the fishing gear ready and mix the gas for the kicker."

Working as a team was part of the fun of living in their remote home. There was always something that needed to be done, and even the simplest chores were best accomplished as a team effort. When firewood needed to be split, two could do it easier than one. Today's trip to the head of the lake would be fun, if they worked together.

Justin pulled the gas can from the Bayliner, and mixed the fuel with two-stroke oil for the small outboard motor they used for trolling. The boat's stern-drive engine would be the workhorse today, but much of the time would be spend travelling slow with the kicker, fishing and enjoying the scenery. At the Head, they planned to stay overnight in the boat, tied up to the logging dock.

The Head was only five miles north of Third Narrows. By the time you travelled all the way to Justin and Ashley's floating home, you were already almost all the way to the Head. Not many people came this far north, so the final stretch was always a joy, particularly if you liked remoteness. But being properly prepared was important, since you'd see few boats other than logging crew boats during such a trip.

Shortly after noon, they pulled away from their dock, motoring slowly out towards the lake's main channel. In the process, they passed near the spot they now called "Whirlpool Alley," always checking it these days for any sign of action. Today they found more movement than any other day except the afternoon of discovery nearly two weeks ago. Currents swung every which way, centered over the location Justin had pinpointed between their cabin and John's across the bay.

The swirling action wasn't just larger; it seemed more confused in direction. Rather than a typical ocean current vortex, the movement seemed haphazard, with radial protrusions that seemed to defy the normal laws of backflows.

For nearly ten minutes, the Bayliner sat near the maelstrom, engine off, while Justin and Ashley simply observed the motion in the water.

"Makes me feel uneasy," said Ashley. "In a superstitious sort of way."

"Superstitious or merely perplexed?" asked Justin.

"A little of both. It's very discomforting to see something so obviously powerful and so unknown in our own backyard."

"Too close to home for me, too," replied Justin.

"I can't help but connect it with that weird star in M82. I know it's completely unrelated, but the two did begin about the same time."

"Whatever's happening in M82 is light-years away, so there's obviously no connection," noted Justin. "The fact they occurred at the same time isn't really accurate. They missed each other by millions of years."

"Good point, but still…"

"It's an absolute fact. What we're seeing in M82 today actually happened 12 million years ago. So the two events can't be related."

"Who says?" countered Ashley

* * * * *

The rest of their day was more relaxed, and the trip to the Head was peaceful and full of fish – five of them, all cutthroat trout, and all released from their hooks to swim again. For most of the trip they trolled slowly, using the 3-horsepower kicker to propel the boat as they fished. They slipped close to the towering waterfalls that tumbled into the lake, powered by the snowfields in nearby mountains. This was the prettiest time of the year at the Head, and Justin and Ashley enjoyed every minute of their journey.

They saw only two other boats the entire afternoon, both of them crew boats, both headed south to Blue Ridge. By six o'clock, they were tied up to the logging dock at the Head, ready for dinner on the aft deck.

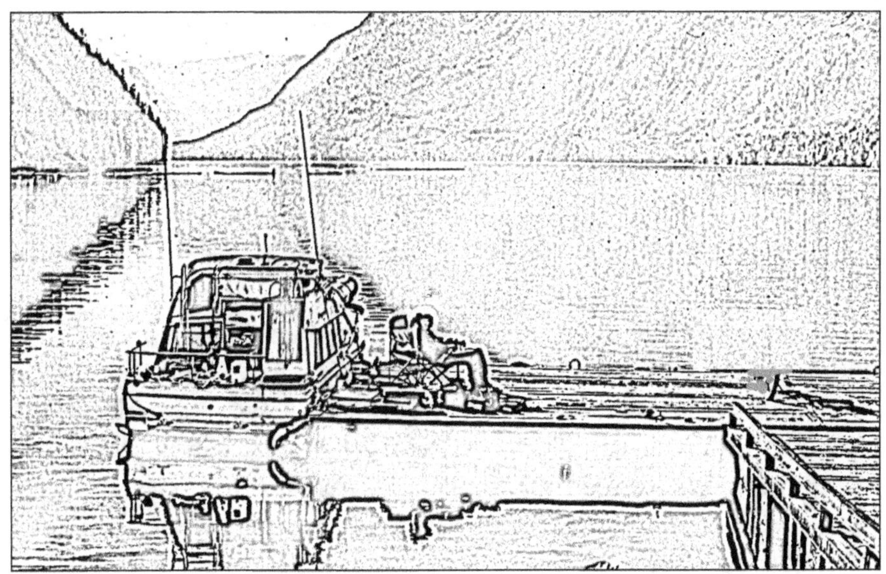

They spent the rest of the evening relaxing on the boat, interspersed with a short hike to the mouth of the river that poured into the lake at the north end. After sunset, the sky glowed bright in the west, then faded to darkness until the first stars appeared overhead. Justin slept soundly in the V-berth, but Ashley got up twice in the night, stepping out onto the aft deck, where she looked up in awe.

Here at the Head, the night sky seemed darker than at Third Narrows. They were even farther from the light pollution of civilization. While she looked up at the stars, Ashley fought back her fright of the unknown.

* * * * *

The next morning, before heading home, they hiked again. This time they walked up the main logging road to a tributary of the river. Here they sat on a rock precipice, watching trout dart back and forth in the stream below. They snacked on granola bars and trail mix from Justin's backpack, and then headed down the road to the boat.

By noon, they were back at Third Narrows, pulling into their beloved bay with their floating home. Something was wrong, but neither of them could quite put a finger on it.

"It's strange, isn't it?" said Justin, before Ashley could express what she similarly felt.

"I don't get it," added Ashley. "Everything looks pretty much normal, but it just seems too bright or something."

When you know a place as well as Justin and Ashley knew their home, you can detect even the smallest change in the environment.

"And it feels funny, like the air is heavy or something," Justin suggested. "Maybe just unusually humid."

Suddenly, while they were looking over their bay, a brilliant flash consumed the entire area. So powerful that, at first, Ashley could only think of a nuclear explosion. In the movies, it was sometimes like that – a brilliant flash from a nuclear bomb that simply consumes everything. Or a super-powerful bolt of lightning. Then, just as suddenly, everything seemed to revert to normal, followed by a strange all-engulfing quiet.

Ashley had turned her head away – it was simply too bright. But now she looked back at the spot where the small whirlpool had been. The odd quiet was replaced by a loud rushing noise, like water gushing wildly out of a pipe too small to contain it.

Between their boat and John's cabin, a gray pillar rose from the water, rapidly climbing like the stem of a nuclear mushroom cloud. It was narrow and smooth-sided, like a thick telephone pole thrusting up into the heavens. Ashley saw where it began on the surface of the lake, but the top was already out of sight, punching through a broken layer of mid-level altocumulus clouds. The pillar didn't bend or waver as it climbed, but just spiked directly upward, puncturing the white clouds and disappearing out of sight.

Then the shock wave hit the Bayliner. It arrived as a loud boom accompanied by a wave almost three-feet high, enough to suddenly rock the boat, and then it was gone. The boat bobbed back down, rebounded a few times without a hint of danger, and settled back to normal. Or as normal as something like this could be.

"Shit!" yelled Justin, the first word either of them had spoken since the sudden blast. "That was amazing!"

It was an understatement, of course, but Ashley was even more affected by what she'd seen. She simply said nothing, but gazed with awe at the towering pillar. It was at least another minute before she attempted to speak — to say anything she could think of, to remind herself she was still alive. But before she could mouth the words, a low-pitched howling noise grew strangely louder, until it engulfed them. And big drops of rain poured down, covering their view in every direction.

"Look at that!" yelled Justin. "The water that went up is already coming back down!"

The gray pillar was nearly transparent now, obviously thinning, but still distinct in front of them. Now rain was pouring down, drenching Ashley and Justin and splashing big drops onto the water around them. It rained for at least five minutes before it stopped. And when it did stop, Ashley noticed the pillar was gone. In fact, all evidence that anything had happened was absent. Their familiar bay had returned to normal nearly as quickly as it had erupted.

This was a moment in time they'd always remember, but maybe never fully understand.

Chapter 9

Reflections of Power

As soon as things settled down – and the water did so amazingly fast – Ashley and Justin considered what they should do. Their first thought was to head for Blue Ridge, check on what was being reported about the explosion, and stay away from Fortune Lake for now. But their home, only a half mile away, looked undamaged and perfectly normal, at least from this distance. The biggest concern, if they stayed here, was whether what had happened might occur again – at any moment.

"This place has never let us down," said Ashley, breaking the silence. "I'm surprised to say it, but I think I'd feel fine staying here tonight. Really, what more could happen?"

Justin gave Ashley a look with raised eyebrows that said: *Well, almost anything.*

Which was exactly the point. There was nothing normal about the explosion that just occurred, but everything seemed undamaged. Was there really any reason to worry further? Sure, their senses were shaken, but the Bayliner was still bobbing in the now-quiet water, totally unscathed.

"Whatever geological forces were at work are gone now, that's for sure," said Justin. "Imagine how much stress must have been relieved in just a few seconds. Similar to how an earthquake relieves the pressure between tectonic plates."

"Maybe it was just that – an earthquake just below the surface, or something similar."

"It must have been geologically extreme, unless there was something underwater that exploded," theorized Justin. "Can't think of anything here though, except possibly an old bomb that ended up in the water but never detonated."

"This is Canada, Justin. Who carries bombs around here."

"Well those fighters from Comox just love to practice over Fortune Lake. You've seen them screaming up the lake. Terrain-following radar practice, I'd guess."

"But bombs?"

"Just thinking out loud, Ash. I really don't have any theory that fits what we saw. So, you're right, let's go home."

* * * * *

They returned to the cabin at trolling speed, now brave enough to drive right past Whirlpool Alley, where no evidence of anything remained. This spot looked no different from anywhere else on the lake, and any residual swirling was gone.

As soon as they pulled into their dock, Justin left Ashley with the job of tying up the boat, while he went inside and came back out with their portable radio. Then they sat on the deck near the boat, their feet dangling down towards the dock, listening to a country crossover tune.

The radio was tuned to the Blue Ridge AM station, which normally provided fair reception this far up the lake. But today's signal was strong.

"Maybe it hasn't made the news yet, but I'm sure they heard the explosion in town," said Justin. "I bet they mention it between songs."

When the tune ended, the radio personality made an announcement about the upcoming garden show at the local hockey arena. Then he introduced the next song. They listened for a few more minutes, waiting for local news on-the-hour. When the news broadcast contained nothing about the explosion, Justin turned off the radio.

"Maybe it wasn't as loud as it seemed," said Justin. "We're a long way from town, and the mountains probably echoed it back to us, and made it seem louder than it was."

"Could be," replied Ashley. "But it must have been loud enough to set off a seismograph somewhere. There'll be something in the *Crier*."

The Blue Ridge *Town Crier* was a weekly newspaper that came out on Wednesdays. It contained a strange mix of local news and Canadian headlines, and seldom missed a chance to cover a story involving anything unusual in the area. Certainly, this incident was big enough to rate major coverage.

"I'd call town and make a report of what happened to the RCMP or somebody," said Justin. "But after that report to the IAU, I don't feel like bothering."

It was in the back of both of their minds, so it was good for Justin to bring it out in the open. There was a strange correlation between the two events, and they happened close together. But how could they be related?

"Anomalies is how I'd refer to them," joked Ashley. "Both occurred at almost the same time, so it seems they could be related. It's just too much of a coincidence."

"But I remind you they didn't occur at the same time," noted Justin. "Remember, whatever we saw in M82 happened millions of years ago."

"Well maybe that star is between us and M82. Maybe it's closer than we think."

"Very possible," replied Justin. "But light from even the nearest star, Alpha Centauri, takes over four years to get here. And the fluctuating star is too dim to be that close."

"You're the astronomer, but I still think it's just too much to happen so close together. I say they're related."

Chapter 10

Localized Events

Things calmed down in Third Narrows again. Nothing more from the whirlpool area, and no fluctuating lights in M82. Even though the sky remained relatively cloud-free for two days in a row, and Justin observed M82 on each of those nights, he didn't detect the fluctuating star again. Observing conditions were nearly perfect, including no winds on the float, which reduced drift in the eyepiece.

On Wednesday, Ashley and Justin went to town to check the *Town Crier* for news about the eruption. But there was nothing in the newspaper even hinting that anything unusual had happened on Fortune Lake.

"Maybe it was so localized that no one was near enough to hear the blast," said Justin. "But you'd think the pillar went so high that someone would have seen it. There's always quite a few logging boats on the lake, and usually several are on the north end."

"So if my theory is correct, and the two events are related, maybe the light in M82 was localized, just like the explosion," suggested Ashley.

As she spoke, Justin thought it sounded like she'd been pondering this for some time. Which she had.

"Now wait a minute. It's simply impossible that a star could only be seen from Third Narrows. Any star among the millions visible through a small telescope is visible everywhere."

"I thought it was billions and billions," quipped Ashley. "But when you say 'everywhere,' I assume you mean worldwide."

"Technically, anywhere in the universe where you're close enough to see it. In earth's case, anywhere on the side of the earth currently in darkness, except for places well south of the equator."

"But if that weren't true — the 'everywhere' part — it would explain why nothing appeared in astronomical news sources regarding such a thing. As you say, amateur astronomers are looking at M82 every night, so someone else should have seen what we saw, but they didn't. Maybe it could only be seen from our cabin."

"That's not the way it works, Ash. If a supernova appears in M82, we would all see it at the same time."

"I know. But maybe this is different."

"It'd have to be mighty different. Because nothing like that has ever happened before, and it never will."

"Mr. Know-it-all." Ashley puckered her lips in her cute girl-like pouty pose, mocking Justin for not giving her idea a chance.

But she'd expected this, and she probably deserved it. Then again, couldn't some localized events be <u>really</u> localized? If it had never happened before, so what? Sometimes when your mind isn't scientifically oriented, you have a lot more room to maneuver.

* * * * *

While they were in town, they both checked their email, finding nothing important, except a message to Justin confirming his parents' plans to visit them in two weeks. It wasn't anything he didn't already know, since Justin and Ashley had invited them over a month ago. But now, with exact dates on the calendar, it seemed more real. They didn't get many visitors, and that was fine with them, so this would be a big deal. They would need to make arrangements to take them up the lake, and back and forth to town so they didn't get bored — unlike Ashley and Justin, who could go up the lake and never feel the need to leave. And there would be elaborate meal plans, and shopping in town in preparation for the visit. Lots to keep their minds off the mysterious anomalies of May.

The somewhat complicated travel plans Justin's parents proposed also involved his brother, Steve. Like Justin, Steve was a pilot, now flying for Alaska Airlines. He owned his own airplane, a Piper Arrow, and he planned to join them in Canada at the end of their parents' visit. It would be quite a family reunion.

Details of Steve's part of the trip, as related to Justin in his mother's message, involved Steve flying to Blue Ridge from Portland in his Arrow just before his parents departed for the United States. They'd all meet in town for dinner, and then Steve would go up the lake with Justin and Ashley the next day. Steve planned to stay for "a few days" (which could mean almost anything, considering his easy-going lifestyle) to explore the backcountry with his brother. The tentative plan was to spend some time on quads, traveling the trails near the head of the lake.

While they sat next to each other in the hotel lobby, Justin forwarded his mother's email to Ashley, the simplest way to explain the details of the upcoming visit.

"Ash, I'm sending you a message from Mom. It'll make you nervous, but I guarantee it will be alright."

Just then, Ashley's laptop beeped, and Justin knew the details were now in front of her. She would be frazzled by the complications of his family's travel plans, but he also knew she would be the perfect hostess – always well organized and ready to please.

In Justin's case, it was almost too much to contemplate. After being alone with Ashley for so long in Third Narrows, his family's visit seemed somewhat like an intrusion. As much as he loved his parents and his brother, he suddenly wished he'd never extended the invitation.

"That's going to be quite a week," remarked Ashley, when she finished reading the email. "Won't be any time to worry about erupting lakes and exploding stars."

"That's the good news," commented Justin. "The bad news is our quiet simple life is about to be shattered."

"Only temporarily, and I'm actually looking forward to it."

"It's a good thing, because it sounds like they're pretty much on their way already, even Steve."

Ashley needed some more time to check her e-book publication sites, so Justin used the opportunity to read several astronomical news bulletins, looking for anything referring to recent M82 reports. He found nothing.

* * * * *

The day after their trip to town, a major storm moved in, and it rained on and off for the next two days. When the sky cleared, Justin set up his telescope on the deck, watching two large groups of sunspots in the afternoon, and inspecting M82 as soon as it was dark. The galaxy was closer to the cliff now. It would still be visible through the end of June, but only in the early evening, so he planned to observe M82 every clear night until then. His interest in the "anomaly" star had become a personal challenge, which was better than the worldwide involvement that Harvard represented. He was much better at private goals than public ones.

When M82 first appeared in the eyepiece, scattered high clouds were moving through that region of the sky. The galaxy was barely visible, to say nothing of the star. But after a few minutes, the clouds moved on, and the star appeared with its normal irregularity – "on" and "off" for a few seconds at a time. Since winds had accompanied the passing cold front, the float was drifting a bit. The image meandered towards the edge of the field of view, and had to be re-centered. After doing this a few times, and verifying the fluctuations were continuing, Justin finally turned his attention to other objects.

As much attention as he was giving M82, he still enjoyed exploring other areas of the sky. On most nights, in more normal times, he would start with "Tonight's Best" in the Astro-Controller, letting the computer decide what he'd enjoy the most. The built-in computer seemed to have a brain in concert with Justin's, since it seldom recommended targets that didn't appeal to him. So tonight, he let it do the thinking.

"Messier 13" was the first item on the "Tonight's Best" list, so he hit Go-To, and the Maksutov-Cassegrain slewed to the right, headed southeast towards the constellation of Hercules. As the scope slowed to a crawl as it eased towards M13, Justin contemplated what he expected in the eyepiece.

This globular cluster was one of his favorite objects, and an observing night seldom went by without viewing M13, if it was adequately above the horizon. Like M82, the image was always exciting; no matter how many times he saw it. With stars packed in such a tight bundle, the

3-dimensional aspect of the object was breathtaking. In his small telescope, he could easily resolve individual stars in the dense cluster's outer area, and they seemed to pop right out at him. Space telescopes could far surpass the detail he saw in his small telescope, but they could never compare to looking at a live image.

When the computer beeped, telling him it was on his target, he approached the eyepiece, and did his best to relax his eye muscles. Peering through the lens, in vivid 3-D, he saw Messier 13 in all its glory. There were moments like this when hauling a bulky telescope in and out of the kitchen was worth all the trouble.

◊ ◊ ◊ ◊ ◊ ◊

Chapter 11

Visitors

When Justin's parents arrived, it was a time of celebration. Jim and Sally knew nothing about the two anomalies that had fascinated Justin and Ashley in recent weeks, and it was best left that way. If they were going to stay overnight for several days in the float cabin, they didn't need to know the place was haunted.

To pick up his parents in town, Justin selected the Campion for the task. This boat was smaller than the Bayliner and less capable in big waves, but it was more comfortable. Usually, the Campion was the boat of choice during the summer, when lake conditions were gentle, while the Bayliner served as the workhorse when the waves got rough. With the weather forecast indicating mild summer-like conditions for his parents' early-June visit, the Campion got the nod.

The 18-foot boat was a bow rider, a design allowing passengers to step through the open center windshield into separate seating in the front. Justin and Ashley preferred to drive this boat with all the canvas removed and the bow fully open. There was nothing Justin liked more than letting Ashley drive so he could kick back in the bow and enjoy the scenery. But it was possible only a few weeks out of the year when the Canadian sun burned high and hot. Most of the time, they configured the boat with the bow covered, and everything else open. For Jim and Sally's visit, it would probably be best to install all of the canvas, including the covering in the rear, and pull it off a piece at a time, if it became warm enough.

The visit was enjoyable for everyone. Sally wasn't accustomed to "camping," as she called it. But she found the cabin a pleasant place to stay. Even the compost toilet was a hit, although Ashley had thought it might be one of the negatives of their visit. Sally probably thought there was merely an outhouse, which was true until only a few months ago. Electricity wasn't a problem (except for the day Sally tried to plug in her hairdryer), since the early-June sun was riding high. And the absence of television forced them to think more about family activities, which was a big positive.

But it wasn't the same in Third Narrows with so many people in one floating cabin. The privacy Justin and Ashley took for granted was shattered, but the tradeoff was some of the best family discussions they'd ever experienced. Sometimes, however, the topics turned in directions that made Justin uncomfortable.

Justin's father didn't understand why his son would chose to leave a lucrative flying career for this, and his mother fretted openly about it. So there was an underlying tension that just wouldn't go away. With Ashley and Justin so firmly ingrained in their off-the-grid lifestyle, they thrived in this floating home. Jim and Sally feigned an acceptance of something they really couldn't fully understand. But they were a family, and it all worked out.

After two days on the float, a day of shopping in town, and then two more days back at Third Narrows, they boarded the Campion for the final trip to town, zooming south to Blue Ridge in only 45 minutes in the speedy boat. Their intricate travel itinerary included a trip to the local airport to meet Justin's brother. When they got there, Steve had just arrived in his Piper Arrow. The timing couldn't have been more perfect.

Everyone in this family loved airports, even Justin's mother, who put up with anything her husband and sons treated as hallowed. And that's the way all three men looked at flying – sacred. Jim had always been an armchair pilot, reading about aviation and talking to his sons about the flying adventures he imagined for decades. Steve, five years older than Justin, took to the skies first, joining the Air Force right after college. He flew fighters, first the F-16 and then the F-22. When he left the Air Force, it was direct to Alaska Airlines for the right seat in a Boeing 737. With his military flying experience, he moved quickly to the left seat, and had been a 737 captain ever since. As Sally reminded Justin, while they bantered over their cups of coffee at the small airport café: "Steve is sure pulling down the big bucks now." Justin took it to mean her short experience with remote living hadn't left a big impression. But he accepted it as lightly as he could, and managed a laugh.

When Justin followed Steve's footsteps in flying, and joined the Air Force, his parents couldn't have been more thrilled. He progressed through military pilot training with fits and starts, but after nearly washing out, he managed to graduate. He asked for fighters, but got the C-130 Hercules instead. He quickly learned to love the Herk, "trash hauling" in the older H-model at first, and then moving up to the glass cockpit J-version. By the time he left the Air Force, he was catching up with Steve in terms of flight experience. Whereas his brother's missions in supersonic fighters were typically an hour at a time, Justin droned on for long legs overseas, logging flight time at an amazing clip.

His job with Boeing was a natural for a guy with extensive military experience in transport aircraft. Still, it wasn't quite where he wanted to be. When it came time to leave the big factory in Seattle, he never looked back. He hadn't logged a single flight hour since then, and didn't regret it a bit. Still, when he saw Steve's Piper Arrow, a familiar longing returned to his soul. Maybe he could get some flight time over the next few days.

That evening, Justin's family (including Ashley, of course) celebrated their Canadian get-together over dinner at the marina pub. They all stayed overnight at the hotel, rising early to drive Jim and

Sally to the airport to catch the commuter flight to Vancouver. As their visit ended, it was all hugs and kisses. The three "kids" smiled and waved while Jim and Sally walked to the intrinsically ugly but aerodynamically efficient Flying Boxcar.

On the drive back to the marina, Justin gave out an audible sigh of relief, kidding Steve that their parents were "always fun, but always demanding."

There would be unspoken contentment the next few days, quite different from the previous week. Steve and Justin always got along famously, and they shared a lot of personal characteristics. They also shared physical similarities, including bone structure in their arms and legs, which were neither muscular nor flabby, but hinted at athletic prowess. And when they smiled, you could see it in their faces – they were brothers.

Steve, like Justin, was an outdoors kind of guy, and he was thrilled to have the chance to experience Third Narrows. He loved boats as well as planes, and looked forward to some backcountry adventures on an all-terrain vehicle. There was little specifically planned, which is the way they all preferred it. When he was away from the airline, Steve was purposefully undisciplined with regards to day-to-day plans. He came to Blue Ridge with no specific schedule, and that was just fine as far as both brothers were concerned. Ashley, too, felt comfortable around Steve. She particularly liked seeing Justin enjoy his brother's friendship, and she knew she wouldn't be left out of their adventures the next few days.

There was, however, the limitation posed by the number of ATV's stored on the old logging road behind the cabin. Both Ashley and Justin rode their own quads, and now there were three people. Of course, one of them could "double" on the back, and that would be Ashley. She didn't like it, however, never feeling comfortable on a quad when she wasn't in control. So the two brothers would get some bonding time without her.

They'd go flying in the Arrow without her, too, because she frankly didn't have an interest in it. She was definitely a backwoods kind of girl these days, and her interests didn't stray very far. She looked forward to some time alone on the float while Steve and Justin took to the winding trails and uncongested skies.

The closeness of the two brothers brought a special benefit to Justin and Ashley during this unusual time in their life. The two anomalies were something they had, so far, kept to themselves. Now Justin felt comfortable sharing them with Steve. His older brother was interested in science, having majored in physics in college. He didn't have the same personal passion for astronomy, but he was certainly looking forward to seeing the deep sky through a Maksutov-Cassegrain.

Their first night together on the float brought clear skies. Justin showed Steve how to align the telescope – tonight using Arcturus and Vega, since Regulus was now riding too low in the evening sky.

"Arc to Arcturus," said Justin.

"I remember that from our camping days, fishing with dad," replied Steve, following the arc of the Big Dipper's handle to the bright orange star.

"There it is!" said Steve.

"I want to show you M82 as soon as it's dark enough," said Justin. "It's a galaxy that's been getting a lot of my attention lately."

Then he seized the chance to bring his brother up to date on the M82 anomaly, trying to keep it simple, telling him only that there was a blinking star near the galaxy. Steve was fascinated, and not a bit skeptical.

With the alignment complete, but still not dark enough for deep-sky objects, they stepped back into the cabin to join Ashley. Over a hot chocolate, they talked further about the blinking star. Justin explained his irregular success in seeing the star on any particular night. Steve was intrigued.

Then, in passing, Justin mentioned the exploding pillar, and Steve gave him a blank stare that said: "Now wait a minute…"

Justin thought it was best to go one step at a time, so he backed off, and said: "Let's talk more about this later." Maybe he was leaning towards Ashley's view regarding a common thread between the fluctuating light and the explosion on the lake, even though he didn't realize it.

When it was adequately dark, all three of them stepped out onto the deck to try their luck at the eyepiece. It was perfect observing conditions – clear, with no wind to sway the float. But they saw no fluctuating source of light in M82.

However, the night was far from wasted. With M82 still an interesting object to explore, Steve was thrilled to observe it "live." When he said he'd seen enough, Justin switched over to "Tonight's Best" in the Astro-Controller, and selected "Messier 13." He hit the Go-To button, and slewed his trusty telescope to M13, the globular cluster in Hercules.

"Just beautiful," said Steve, with an honest sense of wonder in his voice.

Chapter 12

Convergence

The three of them spent the next day enjoying life at the floating cabin. They climbed the trail to the quads, refueled them from a 5-gallon can, and talked about their plans for riding later in the week. Then they hiked to an old logging slash, where they shared a pair of binoculars to watch the seemingly-infinite variety of birds flittering from stump to stump.

In the afternoon, they took a ride in the tin boat. Ashley drove, since this was her favorite, a small vessel she used for exploring around the bay.

She pulled the handle of the starter cord with as much muscle as she could muster, and the 15-horseboard outboard motor came to life on the first try. When the engine was warm enough to close the choke, she nodded to Steve to disconnect the mooring line at the bow. She unhooked her own line at the stern, and gave the dock a push to launch them away from the cabin. Then she shifted into forward gear, and they were off.

By the time they motored a short distance from the breakwater, they were approaching the location where the pillar had gushed into the sky, so she punched the stop button, and let the tin boat drift over the exact spot. The water wasn't disturbed at all now, so they floated in the hushed quiet, engine off and talking softly about what had happened here. Steve seemed to comprehend, and he didn't even question their sanity.

"Well, I can't completely imagine it, since it was such a strange occurrence, and I wasn't here," explained Steve. "But I do understand it, in a fundamental sort of way. The earth is alive with activity under the surface, although we seldom witness it, so why not under a lake?"

"It's nice to be able to talk to someone who can accept what we saw," said Ashley.

"Well, it's not just because I'm your brother," replied Steve, looking directly at Justin. "I understand science, at least at a basic level, and I know there are forces like this that occasionally blast their way out of the earth. Geysers are an example."

"It was like a geyser," agreed Justin. "But so sudden and so immensely powerful. You should have seen that pillar."

"I wish I had. The fluctuating star, too. They could be related."

"That's what Ashley says," replied Justin. "But I don't think so. You do realize they aren't even in the same time zone, don't you?"

"You mean the delay in the light from the star. It would be years in transit, of course, and a lot longer if it's coming all the way from M82."

"So with a background in science, you'd have to say they can't be related," countered Justin.

"Technically, yes. But there are lots of things we don't know, and this might be one of them. You heard about the big discovery at the CERN labs last year, I assume."

"Sure," replied Justin. "The bit about the tachyons, or something that acts a lot like a tachyon. A particle travelling faster than light still seems vague, and it wouldn't apply to light from a star, or from anything that shines."

"Vague, maybe," said Steve. "But we still don't really understand light, even though we've been dealing with it for eons. Remember Einstein's dilemma? – It's a particle; no, it's a wave; no, it's a particle. Why couldn't light, in certain forms, be an instantaneous thing?"

"Well, it's contrary to what Einstein said, and he was pretty smart," replied Justin.

"But nobody knows everything that goes on in this universe. Nobody."

Chapter 13

Whirlpools and Serendipity

The sky remained relatively clear, with a scattering of high cirrus clouds, an indicator of an approaching storm. The evening conditions were barely adequate for the Maksutov-Cassegrain, considering the reduced visibility, occasional obscuration by the high clouds, and a pickup in the wind. Although the cabin was swinging noticeably, Justin set up the telescope anyway.

Success! Regardless of the deteriorating sky conditions, the fluctuating light popped into view, demonstrating its normal oscillating antics. When Steve saw it, he was appropriately impressed.

"Just like you described. The big question is can we correlate it to anything."

"Meaning why that star fluctuates tonight but not last night?" asked Justin.

"If it's a star – and I don't buy into that totally – how does tonight differ from any other night?"

It was delightful to have another mind at work on this mystery. Having another pseudo-scientist on the job thrilled Justin. And that's how the brothers could best be described in this case – amateurs trying to solve a professional astronomer's mystery.

"How about the weather conditions?" suggested Justin.

"That's the kind of thing I mean, but don't forget other factors could be different, although they don't seem related in any way. Heck, it could be something as simple as the time of day."

Later that night, over a shared bowl of popcorn, Justin, Steve, and Ashley talked further about possible relationships between the fluctuating light and changing conditions at the cabin.

"The weather conditions seem backwards," noted Ashley. "When it's super-clear, you never see the object. But on nights like tonight, when conditions are marginal, there it is."

"That's contrary to what you'd expect, that's for sure," said Steve. "But maybe it has to do with the wind. You mentioned it never seems to appear on calm nights."

"But that's backwards, too," offered Justin. "Calm nights are better for observations, because the float isn't shifting around constantly."

"Well, here's a theory for you," stated Steve, ever so slowly. "What if movement of the float foundation coincides with fluctuations of the light? That is, when the float moves, the light twinkles."

"I don't get what you're driving at," said Ashley. "Starlight doesn't depend upon whether the observer is moving or not."

"Is that so?" asked Steve, with a hint of superiority in his voice. "Who says motion has nothing to do with what you see? In fact, even Einstein says otherwise."

"But Ashley's right," replies Justin. "How would it make a light fluctuate?"

"Try this on for size," suggested Steve. "Suppose the light is actually steady all the time? Then your cabin drifts away from the centerline of the beam, and the light goes out. You drift back into the beam, and there it is again."

"Now wait a minute, Steve!" challenged Justin. "That's ridiculous, and you know it! Light from a star is viewed the same over the entire face of the nighttime earth. You can't move only a few feet and see it differently."

"True. But that's for a star or galaxy. Suppose it's some other kind of weird object. And suppose, in fact, it's transmitting a precisely aligned beam aimed extremely close to the cabin, so you drift in and out of it routinely. When the wind blows, the float moves, and you see the light. Drift the other way, and the light seems to go out."

"A laser beam," offered Ashley.

"Like a laser, but maybe something much more sophisticated. The beam could be carrying information down to the lake, or up from the lake, for that matter."

"Now I get where you're going with this," said Justin. "The swirling mass out there is receiving a laser-like flow of light or sending out a beam. And we drift in and out of the stream of light."

"Exactly," replied Steve.

"Beam me up Scotty," added Ashley.

* * * * *

The next morning, before Justin and Steve were awake, Ashley pulled the starter cord on the outboard, and motored out in her tin boat to check the whirlpool. Halfway to the spot, she could see it roiling, small sticks corkscrewing slowly in a wide circle.

She pulled up close, and shut off the engine. Her little boat drifted off to the side of the whirlpool on its own, and stopped. As Ashley expected, this vortex seemed to have no malicious intent as far as she was concerned. She could sit and watch it as long as she wanted.

Here was part of the answer. Maybe.

The whirlpool was active this morning, just as she expected. The previous evening's fluctuating light might have been a beam of information from the viewpoint of the whirlpool. And as best as she could remember, the only time they saw the churning swirl was when they also saw the fluctuating light. They were related. And if they were related, the mystery was actually simpler. There was only one anomaly at Fortune Lake.

◊ ◊ ◊ ◊ ◊ ◊

Chapter 14

The Harsh Realities of Life

When Justin and Steve plopped down at the picnic table for breakfast, Ashley had already returned from her ride in the tin boat, and ready to contribute her meager cooking skills to the morning meal. She'd already prepared coffee, and was now finishing up her attempt at a big omelet that looked a lot like scrambled eggs.

"Is eggs and toast enough this morning?" she asked, as Steve gratefully reached for his freshly-poured cup of coffee.

"Sounds great," answered Steve.

"Me, too," added Justin.

The two brothers planned to get away early, headed to town in the Campion to go flying in the Piper Arrow. Justin was thrilled to have a chance at the controls, and Steve was enthused by the opportunity to introduce his brother to his cherished airplane. They'd probably not go far. A few takeoffs and landings is what Justin wanted, and that would be fine with Steve.

An hour later, as they pulled away from the cabin in the Campion, Ashley yelled over the throaty noise of the engine.

"Fly high and fast! And fly careful!"

* * * * *

She knew they would be careful, and they were extremely experienced as pilots. They wouldn't do anything stupid, but still she worried a bit. It was a reminder she was alone in life, were it not for Justin, but it was by choice. Here she was floating around on a lake in Canada, while her husband was screaming around in the sky nearby. What would happen to her if Justin was gone? Could she stay here by herself, or would she simply move out of the wilderness, and return to the norms of society? It was a sobering thought that she pushed aside.

The rest of her afternoon was full of privacy, and she liked that. She worked in her garden, caught up with her writing by self-editing three full chapters for her soon-to-be-released e-book.

For over an hour, she sunbathed on the deck in the warm afternoon sun of early June. Here was a place of complete privacy, especially before the summer inflow of people. She slipped off her T-shirt and shorts, tugged her pony-tale out of her hat, and let her slim body stretch out in the sun, with a feeling of intimacy with the surrounding environment.

By six o'clock, she started to worry. Justin and Steve weren't back yet, though they hadn't promised anything except they'd be home before dark, with a request to "Hold supper for us."

So she prepared a salad, and put it in the refrigerator to chill. The barbecue was ready to fire up on the deck, and three pork chops were marinating on a big platter. She set the table (the picnic table, that is), and waited.

Then, just when real anxiety was beginning to roll in, the sound of the Campion's engine reverberated from the south. This motor was one she heard many times, and she could tell it apart from other boats from at least a mile away. So before apprehension could reach a peak, they appeared around the corner of Third Narrows. Steve was driving, and as soon as they saw her standing on the deck next to the barbecue, Justin started to wave. They were home, and she was a bit embarrassed. Her worries had been for naught.

* * * * *

The next morning began similarly. Ashley took her tin boat out to investigate the whirlpool, and it was gone. The previous night, Justin and Steve couldn't observe M82 because of thick clouds, but she expected they wouldn't have seen the fluctuating light. After all, the vortex wasn't flowing.

Justin fixed bowls of oatmeal with blueberries and walnuts for all of them. They ate at the picnic table, as usual, under a cloudy sky with a threat of rain. But it wouldn't stop them from riding up into the mountains on their quads, as long as it wasn't (as Justin referred to it) "pissin' down rain."

By ten o'clock, Justin and Steve had climbed up the steep stairs behind the cabin, headed for the upper trail and the quads. This was one of Ashley's favorite places to climb, and she momentarily wished she'd decided to go with them. The climb began with an inspirational transition from water to land, across the bridge to shore. Then past the shed and up the stairs to the trail along the cliff, where you could look down on the floating cabin before slipping into the deep woods.

Ashley went back to washing dishes in the kitchen, and tidying up the rest of the downstairs living area. Nothing major, but necessary now and then. What housework she needed to do was best reserved for rainy days, or at least less-sunny days like today, when it didn't take time away from the glorious outdoors.

Compared to the day before, Ashley was much more relaxed. Quads required care in their operation, but they weren't like airplanes. Both Justin and Steve were experience ATV riders, and they were careful how they rode. Riding alone would have been more worrisome, but even then, Ashley didn't worry about Justin when he was alone on his quad, probably because she also rode, and knew quads. Airplanes were a different matter.

While Justin and his brother explored the old logging roads and narrow trails leading to the head of Fortune Lake, Ashley spent another enjoyable day at her cabin.

* * * * *

Soon after cranking up their quads and starting their drive north on the old logging road, they startled a bear grubbing for food in a slash near the road. This was a black bear, posing little danger to people. Grizzly (brown) bears had moved into the more northerly mountains surrounding Fortune Lake in recent years, a product of new power lines crossing the peaks. These new paths for animals brought grizzlies down from the more remote regions, but black bears still ruled this area (cougars, too). A black bear encountered on a quad was little challenge for the rider. But it was always fun to stop and watch for a few minutes.

The bear didn't stay around long, beating a fairly hasty retreat until it disappeared from sight in the nearby trees. This would be the only bear Steve and Justin would see today, but they did find lots of challenges in the terrain. At one spot, they pointed their quads towards a steep incline on a trail curving up a slippery granite slab.

"Better use four-wheel drive on this," hollered Justin over the sound of their engines, as Steve pulled up next to him. "If it gets too steep, stop and engage your lockers."

Differential lock was used only in the most extreme terrain. With the lockers engaged, steering took brute force. Steve was familiar with lockers, because he sometimes used them in his own quad territory in the Cascade Mountains of western Oregon. Today was a day when they might be required again.

"Give 'er shit, bro!" yelled Steve, as Justin pushed his thumb-throttle forward, and started up the hill in four-wheel drive.

* * * * *

Soon after 7 o'clock, about the time Ashley expected Justin and Steve to walk down the steep cliff-side steps from the trail above, she saw a boat come around the point at Third Narrows. It wasn't a boat she recognized at first. Most vessels this far north were larger, usually big welded-aluminum crew boats. This one was smaller, so she watched it closely to see where it was going.

After rounding the point, the little boat headed directly towards her cabin, and she wondered who this might be. Then her heart felt like it would burst from her chest, and she gasped for air. Now she recognized the small craft. It was the inflatable she sometimes saw on the lower lake – the RCMP.

Why would they come here unless they were delivering important news? News so important it shouldn't be delivered over the phone.

They had motored all the way up here from the marina to tell Ashley that her husband was dead.

◊ ◊ ◊ ◊ ◊ ◊

Chapter 15

Reawakening

The sudden shock of that day was a stark memory, now months behind her. Ashley could never put it out of her mind, but she had to if she was to survive. When the cops stepped out of their boat, strong men looking overwhelmingly somber, she knew what they had to tell her. After delivering the news, they offered to stay until she could calm down enough to go to town for the necessary positive identification of a body. The older officer offered to drive her boat, but she declined. She would start her new chapter in life on her own, even if she hated it. Ashley started the engine, and angled out from the dock in the Campion. The inflatable boat and its powerful outboard motor followed respectfully behind her all the way back to town.

Steve had been injured when he went scrambling down the ravine on foot, trying to save his brother, already dead. The rescue team, summoned by Steve, refused to let him come back up the lake to notify Ashley. Instead, he was now in the local hospital, recovering from broken ribs and a dislocated shoulder, caused by his downhill clamber to try to save his brother. When Ashley arrived at the hospital, Steve's condition was listed as "stable."

Ashley stayed overnight at the hotel, while Steve called his parents and broke the tragic news. On her second day in town, Ashley decided to go back up the lake, against Steve's arguments for her to stay with him in Blue Ridge until she was able to function better. Or, as he argued, at least until he could go back to the cabin with her.

But Ashley, still dressed in the *Air Force* logo sweatshirt she'd been wearing when the RCMP appeared in Third Narrows, insisted otherwise. She was a strong woman, even now. She didn't know what she was going to do, but for now she was going to do it alone at her cabin on the lake.

Before driving to the marina, Ashley made a routine stop at her postal mailbox. She might not be back to Blue Ridge for a while, so she really should see what business was waiting for her. Inside the box were their long-delayed Canadian permanent residency cards. She and Justin, after all the waiting and playing of awkward games at the border, were now officially Canadians. She cried as she put the two cards in her pocket. This would have been a happy moment for Justin.

* * * * *

Now, in the middle of February, eight full months after that tragic day, Ashley was still at her float cabin in Third Narrows. It hadn't been easy, but it wouldn't have been easy in any circumstances. If she had been a female, just turned 30, with no encumbrances to bear, it would have been difficult. With no real family left, and her husband dead less than a year, it was almost overwhelming. But here she was. And she was going to make it – somehow.

Ashley was reawakening from an extreme nightmare, one she suffered over and over, and the burden was huge. But she loved this place even more than before. She would just have to learn to love it without Justin.

One of her attempts to change the situation involved reading. Thank goodness for books when it came to a time of crisis. Her mind could barely attend to her day-to-day needs; yet, she could still focus on the written word. And, if the subject was right, it could sometimes sweep her away. Her e-reader was the perfect tool for this, since she could scan for new titles when she went to town, and download them for reading back at the cabin.

As a silent tribute to Justin, she decided to try a new release entitled *Universe in a Time Capsule*. Cosmology was far from her normal interests, but it certainly fell into the category of "change of pace." In the back of her mind was a desire to set up Justin's old telescope, if she could figure out how to use the built-in computer. It was not her area of expertise, of course, but another change of pace that might force her out of these bleak doldrums.

She needed companionship, too, and she needed it now. Thus, along came Cassie, a black Labrador retriever already ten years old and about to be put to sleep at the animal shelter. Ashley rescued Cassie during a quick visit to see what dogs were available. It was love at first sight.

Now the dog went with her everywhere. If there was a place Cassie couldn't go, Ashley simply didn't go there. Justin would have liked the name she chose for the dog, for she named the Lab after Casseopeia, the W-shaped constellation of the northern sky, a close friend of Ursa Major, the Big Dipper, and thus a friend of M82.

Selecting a dog was a good first step. Second step – she needed to find help. Physical help, that is, since life in a float cabin requires work, and some of the tasks were beyond her abilities. In some instances, it was merely physical strength she lacked for the tasks that needed to be done. Splitting wood, for example, was something not easily accomplished by a 125-pound woman with the frame of a young girl.

In other instances, it was knowledge she lacked, and it wasn't the kind of thing you could learn in books or on the Internet (even if you had the Internet). Every so often, the cabin or one of her accompanying small floats need new barrels, or the current 55-gallon drums required inflation again to keep the deck level. How do you do that if you're a willowy female? "How" in both physical terms and how-to terms. She needed someone to help.

John was the perfect answer. He had helped Justin and her many times before. His cabin across the bay was a rental, occupied only during the summer, but John routinely travelled the lake end-to-end, beachcombing and "checking things out." As John would say: "I was just checking things out, and stopped in to see if you need any help."

So he'd stop in to visit, ask if there was anything he could do, spend as long as necessary to assist with things, and then motor over to his cabin to inspect its condition. While he was over there, you'd hear the sound of his chainsaw as he cut firewood, or the pounding of a hammer as he fixed what needed to be fixed.

As strong as Justin had been, he lacked remote living know-how. John helped with the replacement of the thick steel cables connecting the cabin to the shore. And he knew how to put barrels underneath, and how to inflate them.

So after Justin's death, Ashley went to John. More specifically, John came to her a few days after that fateful visit by the RCMP. He pulled in past Third Narrows in his 17-foot Hourston, his big Yamaha outboard throttled back as he approached her cabin. When he docked his boat by precisely kicking the ass around, as he always did with such perfection, Ashley knew help had arrived. He offered before she could even ask. She hired him on the spot – a more regular schedule than before, at an hourly rate plus travel time from the marina.

Now John was on a schedule that never failed unless a storm moved through the region. He'd arrive at about 11 o'clock in the Hourston every Monday and Thursday to check things out and determine what needed to be done. Most of the time, Ashley had jobs waiting for him, but if she didn't have anything that day, they'd sit at the picnic table (or, in winter, on the old yellow-flowered couch), munching on peanuts and drinking pop.

Then, before John left, he'd always do something, even if there was nothing that needed doing. Some days he'd go out to the floating woodshed and split a few logs. Or he'd take the engine cover off the tin boat's 15-horse motor and clean the spark plugs. Then he'd go over to his Hourston, start the engine, and wait several minutes before leaving the dock to assure his old motor was properly warmed. Usually, once the engine was ready, he'd head slowly across the bay to check things out at his cabin, maybe sweep off the deck or pound a few nails. Sometimes, if it was getting late, he'd just make a sweeping glide past his cabin in his boat. Then he'd take the Hourston up on plane, and angle straight out towards the narrows, headed back down the lake to town.

Without John, she couldn't have stayed here. But with him, she was ready for whatever life might throw her way. She kept all of the boats. The Bayliner was a good backup for the Campion during rough weather, although she didn't like driving it as much as the sporty 18-footer. She kept the quad that survived the accident, and rode it regularly by herself, being careful where she went, but never worrying about her fate. She'd driven Interstate 5 through Seattle for years. Neither airplanes nor quads could equate to that level of danger. Justin had died on a quad, but it could as easily have been an airplane, a truck, or even coming down the stairs from the loft.

If you were determined to claim a slice of paradise, you had to take risks. Seldom does a baseball player steal second base without taking a big lead off first.

* * * * *

Ashley turned around from the sink, pausing as she washed the dishes. She stared at the open pantry shelves. It was bothering her. The thin plywood panels that Justin had installed were sagging in the middle. All three shelves curved downward at the center, looking sloppy and disturbing her sense of order. It was unimportant, which is why Justin had never fixed it. But now, after months of hefty pantry supplies – mason jars of blackberry jam, 2-kilogram bags of sugar, big jars of peanut butter – the shelves drooped too far, and distracted her.

She turned back to the dishes, drew a hefty stream of water from the hand pump in two quick strokes, and then reached for the towel. She dried her hands, and headed for the door.

Outside on the porch, Ashley paused and scanned her "front yard," where her floating garden sat along the log breakwater. Low stratus clouds pushed up against the cliffs of Third Narrows, in typical majestic beauty.

She paused briefly, and then walked determinedly to the stash of lumber stored under the deck near the Bayliner. She poked through the pile until she found three long pieces, one-by-two's that would work for shelf supports. Then she went back inside to find the measuring tape, a felt pen, and the handsaw. Using these tools, she placed the first piece of wood on the bench of the picnic table, where she could hold it tight using her foot as a vise.

Then she went back into the kitchen, using the tape for the measurements she needed, and returned to the picnic table to cut three short segments to be used as braces for the shelves.

When she was done, Ashley slid the wood posts into position, and the thin plywood shelves sat level and comfortable to her eye. Then she went back to the sink, and finished the dishes.

Tomorrow she'd ask John to show her how to use the chainsaw. He'd hesitate, worried about her safety, but then he'd give in and show her what she needed to know, and where to be careful. She'd pay close attention, and smile thankfully as John explained how to cut firewood.

* * * * *

In Third Narrows, life slowly returned. It could never be the same, of course, but life would go on. And Ashley would be here to enjoy it. Ashley thought about selling Justin's cherished Maksutov-Cassegrain telescope, but she realized it was as much a monument to Justin as anything else in the house. It could remain in the kitchen as either a disturbing reminder of her loss, or she could embrace it, putting it to use in the night sky. After all, she still had a mystery to solve. Justin would have never let those anomalies – or was there only one? – get away from him. Even if he couldn't solve a mystery, he would have never stopped trying. Now it was her job to take over.

As part of her increased pace of reading, Ashley embraced Justin's astronomical volumes that rested on the bookshelf. When she went to town for a dose of Internet at the hotel lobby, she added a special edition of *Scientific American* to her e-reader – a series of articles regarding the wonders of the universe. She stumbled with the terminology, and had to skip over most of the equations, but she actually understood a lot of what she read. On many evenings, she'd curl up on the couch with her e-reader, looking out over the tranquil lake, and watching the embers in the fireplace die as the clock slipped past midnight.

So one night in late February, when the sky finally cleared after a full week of nearly constant pissin' down rain, she hauled the telescope out onto the deck. She slipped the hydraulic pads under the tripod legs, just as she'd seen Justin do. She set the date and time on the rotating star chart (or "planisphere," as Justin always called it), and picked two bright stars for alignment that she could easily identify – Capella, nearly overhead, and Rigel, above the southern horizon. Then she went through the alignment process, using the set of instructions from the operating manual. She'd seen Justin do this many times, and she beamed with pride when she received an "Alignment Successful" message from the Astro-Controller on her first try.

M82 was the obvious target. Tonight it was just rising above the cliff to the north, riding out front of the bowl of the Big Dipper. The observing position was ideal, and M82 would be rising higher for several hours, as the Big Dipper stood on its handle.

On the Astro-Controller, Ashley selected "Deep Sky," then "Messier Objects," and finally "Messier 82." The Go-To button took her promptly to the cigar-shaped galaxy, now tilted at a different angle than in June. The fluctuating light came into view almost immediately, and then winked off.

As she held her eye to the 17-millimeter eyepiece, M82 floated to the left. She looked away from the telescope to watch the deck slowly shift towards the shore.

"Check! – image fluctuating, float moving," she said out loud, as if speaking to Justin. Cassie barked twice (*Woof, woof!*), reacting to Ashley's voice.

She'd taken her tin boat to Whirlpool Alley many times since Justin's death – every time she went to town – and on most days, it was stagnant. But this afternoon she had gone there again, in anticipation of tonight's experiment. The whirlpool was spinning, and now the light was fluctuating.

"Check! – image fluctuating, whirlpool whirling," she chimed, although no one was listening but Cassie, who barked again: *Woof, woof!*

Tomorrow she'd do something about those three things – image fluctuating, float moving, whirlpool swirling – although she wasn't yet sure what.

Chapter 16

Sub Chaser

Ashley smiled to herself, one of those rare times since Justin disappeared from her life. There was a correlation in the two anomalies, or certainly there might be. To heck with theories involving the speed limit of light. She was onto something, and it felt good.

Now how to get the help she needed. She was neither a scientist nor a person anyone would listen to, unless she had a pretty good story. So she made one up.

"Hello, I'd like to speak to the base publicity officer," she said into the phone.

The telephone operator put Ashley's call through, letting her know they called that office "Public Information" on this base. She was quickly connected, but then realized she was speaking to just a clerk. So she tried to weasel her way into speaking to someone who was more authoritative by using some fancy terms she'd heard Justin use many years ago when he was fresh out of the Air Force.

"Could I speak to the OIC? Or the NCOIC, if he's not available," she said with a sense of command.

"I'm not sure who you mean," replied the clerk. "Oh, officer-in-charge. We don't call him that. It's an American term. But Lieutenant Formosa is standing in for our boss today, though he's on the phone to his wife right now."

"That's okay. I'll hold."

A mere lieutenant in anyone's military, Canadian or otherwise, didn't sound very powerful, and what about an office that tells you he's on the phone to his wife? Well, you had to start somewhere.

When the lieutenant came on the line, he was a joy to deal with. He tried to act official, but he didn't pretend to be powerful. In a nutshell, he seemed sincerely cheerful, and Ashley could use a touch of that.

"Not sure we had any report of any kind of an explosion over there. At least not since I've been in this department."

"And how long have you been in public information?"

"About three months," he replied. "I wanted to be assigned to air traffic control, but they're full right now."

"Oh. Well, let me try to explain the details regarding this explosion, and maybe you should tell someone higher up the ladder."

"I can do that, 'mam."

She hated the term "'mam," but she needed his help. And he was pleasant enough. So she gave him as many details of the explosion as she thought necessary, and even tried to add some extras that might get his attention.

"I think it might have been a bomb, maybe something dropped from one of your aircraft on a training mission, and it exploded right here in the lake."

Silence. Now that seemed to get his attention. Maybe he had pulled out a notepad and was taking notes.

"Er, we don't carry armed weapons on training missions, 'mam."

"Are you sure?" She pouted her lips, though she knew no one could see.

More silence. He probably wasn't sure.

"Well, I'll let the captain know about your call as soon as he comes back."

A captain was certainly a higher rank, but not much above a lieutenant in the U.S. Air Force. But a lot higher if Canadian pay grades were like the Navy.

"Here, I'll give you the coordinates so you can check it out. The specific date was May tenth of last year, and I think something is still down there, maybe ready to explode again."

"Now how do you know it might explode?" chided the lieutenant, with a higher pitch in his voice.

"I've done some investigating," replied Ashley. "Not the kind of professional stuff you do, of course, but I've had friends help me with an underwater camera and some chemical samples, too."

"Really? Now I'm going to pass this on to the captain, although you really haven't got any photos or chemical evidence, do you?"

"I'm working on it."

"Give me the coordinates, and I promise I'll pass them on."

A pledge from this cheerful fellow was worth taking a chance. Ashley read the coordinates to him from her GPS. Then she said she hoped he got that job in air traffic control, and she meant it. He thanked her with one last "'mam" before hanging up.

* * * * *

She now had a theory, and it was close to ridiculous. But at least it was something that could be proved or disapproved, which was paramount to the scientific method.

Suppose there was something either alive or robotic underwater. Why it had picked this location didn't really matter, although the lake is remote, which might be a factor. If it were associated with alien life, then it would need to communicate with its home. Which might explain the light beam.

Of course, using light itself would be inefficient, but where there's light there's other wavelengths, especially on the red end of the spectrum – microwaves, X-rays, you name it. The problem of timeliness remained, since any signal sent from (or to) space would suffer communication delays. In the case of M82, that would mean waiting 12 million years. (Do you need another bottle of milk? Let me know in a few million years.)

Then again, it was like Steve had said – there really aren't any standards here, and there's a lot we don't know. Even scientists admit the whole issue of faster-than-light is open to question. Einstein, knowing what we know today, would readily agree.

Then there's the issue of localized effect. How could a beam of energy (light or otherwise) be visible to Ashley, but not seen by telescopes somewhere else? The answer, of course, was some type of laser-like light not yet invented — light rays so compact and parallel that they even exceed the "collimated" light of a modern laser. In current technology, a laser beam would be visible a long distance from its target. If nothing else, the earth's atmosphere would refract some of the light so it'd be visible as a shaft-like beam when viewed anywhere nearby. Light more fully collimated than that was simply unheard of.

Finally, there was the issue of what really happened when the explosion occurred. Ashley assumed the discharge was from the water to the sky, but could it have been the other way around? That is, was the pillar sending a signal (or some aliens) upward, or was someone up there sending something to the bottom of the lake. Maybe it could work both ways, like whales using sonar to communicate.

"Far out!" said Ashley out loud, heard only by Cassie, the birds, and any other critters within shouting distance of the floating cabin.

Woof, woof! responded Cassie.

* * * * *

Aircraft routinely buzzed low over Third Narrows. Sometimes, it was a seaplane hauling logging officials to and from the head of the lake. Often it was a helicopter based in Blue Ridge on a logging run, carrying people or supplies. And sometimes, fighters from Comox flew over the lake, using it for low-level terrain avoidance training. But Ashley had never seen an Orion here before.

The first time it came over, it was headed south, right down the lake but slightly off the west side of Third Narrows, which placed it right over her cabin at an altitude of about a thousand feet. Before she saw it, she heard the powerful engines, four T56 Allison turboprops mounted upside-down on the wings. She remembered Justin telling her the Orion had its engines wrong-side-up. Of course, that's because his cherished Air Force C-130 used the same Allison engines, mounted right-side-up. The Navy and the Air Force never got along.

At their old home in Seattle, P-3 Orions would often fly overhead on their way to Whidbey Naval Air Station. Ashley remembered the plane, and she even remembered the droning sound of those four turboprops. This airplane was definitely a P-3 with its distinctive protruding tail "stinger." She'd never seen Orions here before. They were full of high-tech electronic equipment, and their primary mission was chasing subs. She knew why this one was here.

After that first pass, she watched the big airplane swing around the mountains to the east, climbing to safely clear the rough terrain. Then the pitch of the engines dropped, as the aircraft descended again, just out of sight behind the peaks. She caught sight of the P-3 as it dropped even lower, now coming out of a left turn to the north and lining up for another pass. This time it was so low that it disappeared behind the steep cliff that bordered her cabin on the north side. Then, suddenly the Orion burst over the rock wall with a roar of turboprops, passing straight overhead and out over Whirlpool Alley. Then it disappeared to the south.

When the sound didn't return, she looked out at the spot where the whirlpool occasionally swirled. From where she stood on the deck, she could never be sure, but she thought the vortex was beginning to spin.

* * * * *

"**H**ello, I'm Captain Sterling," said the deep voice on the phone, sounding young but experienced. "Lieutenant Formosa talked to you on Tuesday, and I'd like to follow up on your report."

She wanted to ask whether his rank of captain was similar to the Air Force (lowly) or the Navy (powerful), but then she thought it was unnecessary. The important thing was that something was happening, and she was grateful. What did it matter who was driving the bus?

"Hello, captain. Thanks for calling. I saw your P-3 yesterday."

"So you're up there right now?"

"This is where I live."

"Wow! How cool."

Cool was one way to describe it. Yes, living here was mighty cool. And maybe Ashley had misjudged how much fun it might be to work with the military on this. It was almost exciting, and she could use a little levity in the midst of tough times. "Fun" and "happy" seemed like new words to her, and she was glad to welcome them back.

"Mrs. Cambridge, let me bring you up to date," he said. "First, thanks for reporting the explosion. We checked with seismology offices around the province, and they did detect a quake-like disturbance on May tenth, just as you described. It was below the threshold that would normally be reported to anyone, since we get mini-quakes all the time. But it definitely happened. And they could pinpoint it to the coordinates you provided."

She could have screamed with joy, but she kept her composure. It didn't matter that the captain couldn't see her huge smile.

"Oh, good. I was hoping you could help. I really didn't know what to do, but it seemed important. And please call me 'Ashley'."

"Well, it might be important, Ashley. Very important," he said, not offering his own first name. "Our aircraft got some good data on its second pass yesterday. Even the first circuit was amazing – they picked up some stuff we've never seen before."

"What kind of 'stuff' do you mean?"

"Okay, let me get right to the point, 'mam."

"Don't call me that!" interrupted Ashley abruptly.

In quick reaction to Ashley's raised voice, Cassie immediately let out two barks: *Woof, woof!*

"Oh, sorry. I didn't mean to offend you. Was that a dog I heard?"

"Yes, it's my dog."

"I guess 'mam' isn't the best term, is it? I'll try to be careful, but sometimes it just pops out."

"No big deal. I really do appreciate everything you're trying to do. And your lieutenant was helpful yesterday. Please thank him for me."

"There's something I should tell you before we proceed any further," said the captain solemnly. "Lieutenant Formosa works in the public information office. I've probably confused you, since his boss is also a captain, but I'm not in the same office. I'm in charge of the military intelligence unit."

"Oh."

This was probably good. Or was it bad?

"We talked at a meeting here yesterday about what happened on your lake. Let's just say that all of the important people on this base were at the meeting. It's pretty much unprecedented, but we've decided, at the highest levels, to bring you in on our plans. Now you don't work for me, so all I can really do is plead with you to give us all the information you can – complete and accurate data. We need it. In return, I promise to keep you informed of things along the way."

"That seems more than fair. I'll make sure I provide the best information I can, and I won't hold anything back."

"Okay, so let me first explain that I won't be able to tell you much. It probably doesn't make sense to you, but we have a very important job to do, and it could be compromised if anyone knew exactly what type of equipment we have aboard our aircraft. Some of it is top-secret, and just telling you what we found could indirectly identify what type of equipment we're using. Does that make any sense?"

"Absolutely. I understand perfectly what you're saying, and I'm just grateful you're even communicating with me. I don't need to know all the details, but I'll be grateful for anything you can share with me."

"That's only fair," replied Captain Sterling. "I promise to keep you updated. The airplane we're using isn't actually a P-3. It's a Lockheed CP-140 Aurora, which is a derivative of the P-3 Orion. And wave to those guys – they love it, although they're pretty busy pinging."

She wasn't sure what "pinging" meant, but she was grateful for the phone call. The information Captain Sterling provided was more than Ashley had hoped for. He explained the electronic signals from the lake (at the precise GPS coordinates she provided) indicated that sophisticated high-tech gear was down there. It was so high-tech they hadn't a clue (yet) what it was. Now that was quite an admission. Ashley was surprised (and pleased) the captain was willing to divulge even that much. It certainly didn't jive with all she had heard about the military. Then again, both Justin and Steve were former Air Force officers, and they were very straightforward about everything. But she thought it was only because they were "ex-military."

"There will be another airplane today at about 3 o'clock. It'll probably make about 4 passes. Hope we don't disturb the neighborhood."

"Have at it! I look forward to seeing your Aurora."

"Actually, it won't be our airplane. They're sending a P-3 from the States today. They have different equipment. We're working closely with them to make sure we have the best tools for the job. Besides, our Auroras are tied up on something else."

So was this an admission that the U.S. had more sophisticated equipment ("different equipment") or a reminder that Canadian sub chasers were "tied up" on more important work? What did it matter? The anomaly was getting the attention it deserved, fluctuating star or no fluctuating star. Which reminded her of something.

"You've been really truthful with me, so let me tell you one further detail," she said slowly.

"I'm listening."

"Well, there may be something else going on here related to the underwater mystery."

"I like mysteries. At least most of the time."

"It has to do with a beam of light that might be coming from a star or even a galaxy. It's something I've been watching here through a small telescope, and it seems to be flickering on and off. It might be related."

She waited patiently for his reply. This might be too much, and she could have overstepped her bounds. A crazy lady who lives alone on the lake calls to report underwater bombs and a big explosion. Oh, and she's seeing flickering stars that are somehow related to all this.

"Well, I don't think that's even close to my area of expertise," said the captain. "But I'd be glad to put you in touch with the astronomical authorities we work with on cases like this."

Cases like this? Surely, this type of thing is rare. But maybe now Ashley will have a professional to talk to about the astronomy side of the anomaly.

"Sure, I'd appreciate that. A name and phone number or email address would be perfect."

"Might be best if they contacted you," said the captain. "By the way, do you have a fax?"

"I barely have electricity."

"Well, I'll need to send you some kind of security nondisclosure agreement. We'll need you to sign it before we progress much further."

"Okay, but remind those scientists that I can't respond to email from up here, so see if they are willing to phone instead."

Whoever "they" are.

"Sure, I'll do that, but one more thing while I'm thinking of it. About those bombs… How about you not mentioning them any more, and I promise to stop calling you 'mam."

* * * * *

That afternoon, Ashley and Cassie were out on the deck well before 3 o'clock. She knew the American P-3 would warn her of its arrival a long way in advance by the sound of its throaty engines. There was something exciting about being able to hear it when still far away.

She wasn't disappointed, because a few minutes before three, she exclaimed out loud (which was happening more often these days): "Here she comes!"

Woof, woof! barked Cassie.

Sure enough, the distant engine noise grew quickly to a roar, as the still-unseen aircraft slid behind the mountains to the east, circling around to line up for a north-to-south pass.

The low-flying P-3 burst over the cliff to the north, passing straight over the cabin at about 300 feet, and out over the spot where the anomaly, whatever it was, sat under Whirlpool Alley. The Orion continued straight ahead, not deviating in heading a bit, rock-steady and pulling directly away from its target.

As the airplane finally turned eastward to circle again and line up for another pass, she imagined the crew inside, the pilots up front and the technical experts in tall-backed seats in the aft cabin, watching over electronic gizmos they couldn't talk about. The plane climbed as it passed behind the mountains, and then reduced power as it began its descent again, circling back to the north and lining up for another run.

Vroom! Just like the first pass, the P-3 appeared suddenly over the cliff, and drove straight overhead. When she looked up, the entire sky was covered with the outline of the big plane.

Once again, the P-3 continued straight ahead, wings level, and then banked to the east for a third pass. This time, when the airplane broke over the cliff, Ashley started shouting, waving her hands over her head furiously: "Hello! And thanks!" she shouted to herself and anyone up there who might be looking down rather than concentrating on their flight instruments or sophisticated equipment as they should. The airplane continued straight ahead, and again turned eastward for what probably would be the last pass over Third Narrows.

Once again, a tremendous roar as the Orion punched into view over the cliff. Ashley waved and shouted again. It didn't matter that no one noticed: "Hello! Thanks for everything!"

Woof, woof, woof!

The P-3 continued on its straight course, as Ashley imagined the crew studying their CRT's and top-secret equipment. Then, less than a mile south of Third Narrows, the airplane rocked its wings. Not just little rocks back and forth, but 30-degree rolls to each side, and then more wide rolls left and right as it pulled up in a screaming climb straight ahead, headed home.

Chapter 17

Telescope Taste Test

Another aircraft came back the next day, this time just before sunset. This airplane sported a Canadian flag logo, so it was an Aurora. The project was getting attention from both sides of the border. When it completed it's fifth pass, it finally exited to the south, once again climbing and rocking its wings in the now-darkening sky. The throttle jocks in both countries must be talking to each other.

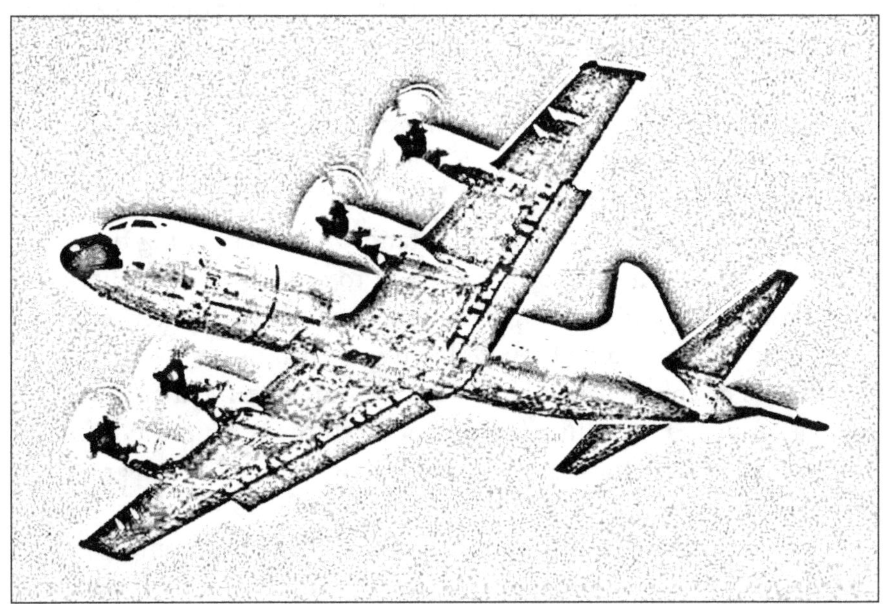

Captain Sterling hadn't called again, but Ashley knew he was on the job. Each time an Aurora came overhead, she uttered thanks to him and the young lieutenant who started the ball rolling. The Orion, predecessor of the Aurora, had recently joined the B-52 bomber as one of only a handful of military aircraft that had served for over fifty years. And like the B-52, the Aurora was now full of electronic marvels that weren't even dreamed of when the airplane was born. A team of sensor operators sat aft of the cockpit, tweaking their computer displays, while simultaneously sending a huge stream of data back to their home base. It was an airborne intelligence lab on steroids.

The phone rang a few days later while she was fixing breakfast. Before answering, she glanced at the clock – exactly 9 am, an indicator someone was afraid to call too early, but wasn't wasting any time.

"This is George Staples," said the gruff voice on the other end. "The International Astronomical Union called me, and asked that I look into your observing situation there in Canada. Is this a good time to talk about it?

"Sure. I appreciate your calling."

"Well, I'm from the University of Arizona, and the IAU has asked me to send some people up there and check out your observatory regarding this fluctuating light source. Could we talk about that?"

"Of course. But I don't have an observatory, just a 5-inch Maksutov-Cassegrain I use for observing on my deck. I live in a floating cabin, so the telescope moves around a bit when the cabin changes positions, and that may be related to…"

"Wait, wait! I'm not sure I understand what's happening there, but if the IAU thinks it's important enough to send a team to check out your observing location, I'll get them headed your way later today."

"Okay, that would be fine. Did you say a team?"

"Only a couple of astronomers, maybe only one and a postdoc, just to analyze things there first-hand. Doctor Thomas from the IAU said you had an observatory. But you say it's just a 5-inch Cassegrain you set up on a deck?"

"Yes, it's a floating deck on a big lake. I'll need to come down to the marina to pick up your team when they arrive, and then we'll load them and their stuff on a boat to bring them back to my cabin. How much equipment do you think they'll have?"

"They'll have to ride in a boat to get to where you live?"

"There aren't any roads."

"Oh, well, it doesn't matter. The IAU is footing the bill."

They're coming all the way to Canada to see a 5-inch telescope sitting in a kitchen. Now that's the kind of action Justin would have appreciated.

* * * * *

The two-man team from the University of Arizona arrived in Blue Ridge two days later, and Ashley met them at the airport. Right away, she could see they were both enthusiastic and knowledgeable. They introduced themselves as Tim Wheaton, a galactic structure specialist, and Jeremy Grimes, assisting Doctor Wheaton on a postdoctoral fellowship. They utilized Kitt Peak's 8-meter telescope for their research, employing spectrometry and gravitational lens technology. Ashley didn't fully understand what that meant, but she liked both of them instantly.

Ashley had filled in Jeremy regarding the details of the fluctuating light during a series of phone calls while the astronomers were changing airplanes in Los Angeles and Vancouver. Jeremy proved easy to get along with. He grew up as an amateur astronomer (and was still growing at the age of 26), using an 8-inch Schmidt-Cassegrain similar to Ashley's smaller Maksutov-Cassegrain. In other words, he really understood Ashley's situation. As he said on the phone from Los Angeles: "What I'd have given for a setup like yours in such a good location."

"The float moves quite a bit on windy nights, so it's a bit of a challenge," she had replied.

"But isn't it usually calm there on clear nights?"

"Normally. But you still need to be careful, even when you walk around on the float, because the telescope drifts when things shift like that."

"It's one of the things we're supposed to look at, according to Doctor Thomas. He's the IAU guy who funded this trip."

"You mean how the movement might affect my fluctuating light source?"

"Exactly. Doctor Thomas thinks it could be an artifact of your Maksutov lens setup – some kind of reflection inside the tube."

Ashley hadn't thought of that. The Maksutov-Cassegrain design includes a correction lens on the very front of the telescope, right where the light enters the tube. Then the light travels down to the main mirror, back to a secondary mirror mounted on the entry lens, and finally the light is reflected back through a hole in the primary mirror and into the eyepiece. That's a lot of places for light to get lost.

Ashley amazed herself that she could think this way. A year ago, she wouldn't have understood anything about how her telescope operated. But Jeremy's suggestion of instrument error was far from appealing.

"You could be coming all the way to Canada just to find I've got a defective telescope. Wouldn't that be a pisser?"

"Yes, it would," laughed Jeremy. "But you know, this has been a fun project so far. Just thinking it through and coming up with theories has been a blast."

Fun? A blast? This whole thing really had been fun since her attitude changed. Making life fun again might not be so hard, after all.

During their last phone conversation, when Jeremy was at Vancouver International, Ashley tried to determine how much baggage she'd need to haul in the boat. The two scientists were traveling with lots of equipment, and a large personal bag for each of them.

Your equipment is designed to test my scope, I assume."

"Yes, but I've also brought along my old LX90. A second telescope should find the same fluctuations, if it sits next to yours and neither of us have erroneous internal reflections."

Ashley hadn't thought of that, but it would be the ultimate test. Two telescopes sitting side-by-side should see the same thing, if it's something real.

"Who came up with that idea?" asked Ashley.

"Me. But the IAU didn't like it. Extra costs for shipping the telescope and tripod. IAU austerity program, you know. But they gave in, and I'll get to show you my Schmidt-Cassegrain."

Just like little kids. Show me yours, and I'll show you mine. They were both having "fun."

But Ashley was still concerned. These two astronomers could easily come all this way and not catch the light fluctuation. It had occurred on only one of three acceptable viewing nights during the past week. And to get adequate sky conditions during the first week of March was asking a lot. Jeremy and Tim would be here for only three days, and the weather forecast didn't look good. Tonight might be acceptable, with partly cloudy skies and 20-knot winds expected. After that, it looked like the sky conditions would go straight downhill. However, if you didn't like the weather forecast around here, wait until tomorrow, and it could change completely.

From the airport, Ashley drove them directly to the marina, which took them through town and it's single stoplight.

"We ain't in Tucson anymore," kidded Jeremy. "Could we make a quick stop at a store where I can pick up some souvenirs?"

"I'm not sure if you're serious. There aren't any tourists here, particularly during March. But if you want something, the best place is probably Canadian Tire."

"Good. Could we go there? I'll be quick"

"The IAU ain't paying for it," joked Tim.

They made a quick stop at the store, located a half-mile past the stoplight. Time was running out, since daylight ends early in March, and Ashley wouldn't take the boat up the lake after dark. Jeremy bought some small Canadian flags on a stick for friends back home and a black *Canada* sweatshirt with red lettering for himself.

At the marina, the astronomers loaded the Bayliner with two big suitcases full of equipment, plus a separate case for the LX90, along with a heavy-duty tripod and their personal bags. Ashley was glad she brought the Bayliner today, both because of the load and in case the storm moved in earlier than expected. She started the engine, and motored out of the marina's log breakwater, headed up the lake with twilight to spare.

Neither Tim nor Jeremy knew much about boats, and they were thrilled about the trip north. While Tim held on tight, Jeremy kept turning around and shooting photos with his cell phone, capturing the always-beautiful spectacle of a boat's wake on Fortune Lake. Cassie, who always enjoyed Ashley's rare visitors, sat beside him, taking it all in.

* * * * *

By the time they unloaded their bags at the cabin, it was already quite dark. But the weather was holding – enough breaks in the clouds that they might be able to catch M82. The wind was gusting rather strong, but even that was a positive. If the light source was going to fluctuate, it should do so on a windy night when the float drifted in and out of range of the supposedly highly-collimated beam.

There wasn't time enough for supper, and Ashley was grateful, because she hated to cook for groups bigger than one. During their travels today, Tim and Jeremy had overdosed on junk food anyway, and she wasn't hungry. But they were all anxious to get started with their telescopes.

The temperature had dropped to 8 degrees Celsius, but that wouldn't be a problem. Jeremy pulled his new *Canada* sweatshirt over his head, and Tim zipped up his jacket. Ashley felt comfortable on the deck with the same sweatsuit she'd fashionably worn to town with her maroon high-top sneakers. Her shirt said *UW Football.* So there they were on the deck, Jeremy with his souvenir Canadian sweatshirt, Ashley dressed like a Huskies jock, Tim like an informal astronomer who was looking for his pipe, and Cassie dressed like a dog.

Jeremy assembled his LX90 a few feet away from the Maksutov-Cassegrain that Ashley brought out from the kitchen. While they waited for the mirrors of both telescopes to cool down to ambient temperature, they went inside to warm up. Ashley served one of her gastronomic delicacies, chips and salsa.

"Just what the doctor didn't order," joked Tim. "But it sure looks good."

They chomped away on the chips and drank root beer.

"This will be a major taste test," said Jeremy. "Schmidt versus Maksutov. And the winner is…"

Ashley laughed, but she hoped there was no winner. What she really hoped is that both telescopes saw a fluctuating star in M82.

* * * * *

And that's exactly what they saw! Two telescopes side by side, looking at the same object, an irregular galaxy in Ursa Major. Two eyepieces simultaneously focused on a faint fluctuating star – "on," now "off," now "on" again.

Ashley shouted in celebration. Tim and Jeremy high-fived each other. Cassie barked: *Woof, woof, woof!*

It was a happy event for all of them. It was fun.

The only thing bothering Ashley and dampening the moment was the third part of the equation. The float had drifted, two telescopes had seen the same fluctuating image, but the whirlpool had been inactive when they arrived at the cabin. Ashley had motored past the area just before they docked, as she always did, to see if it was spinning. It wasn't. Now, three hours later, the light was fluctuating. What was happening to the whirlpool right now? There was only one way to find out.

"Tim, Jeremy – have you ever ridden in a tin boat?"

"You mean an aluminum boat?" asked Tim.

"Yes, it's the same thing."

"Maybe once, a long time ago," said Tim.

"Probably never," added Jeremy.

"Well I'm going out to check the whirlpool, and you're welcome to come along."

"Right now?" asked Tim, with a hint of fright in his voice. "At night."

"I've got lights, and it's only about halfway to that cabin over there." She gestured towards John's float cabin.

Tim and Jeremy knew a little bit about the whirlpool saga, but Ashley doubted they understood what she'd told them. It had been a quick briefing, since the fluctuating light was their part of the mystery. Yet they both had perked up when she told her story: Explosions, crazy woman living by herself in a floating cabin, whirlpools, sub chasing airplanes.

"I'd better stay here," said Tim without hesitation.

"I'll go!" chimed in Jeremy.

"How about you, Cassie?" joked Ashley.

Woof, woof! It was a mute point – Cassie was going whether she wanted to or not.

It took only a few minutes to don their lifejackets and launch the tin boat. The trip was short, barely outside the log breakwater. It wasn't often that Ashley boated on this lake at night. It just wasn't worth the worry. But tonight the trip was short. Then again, they were traveling to a whirlpool with who-knows-what underwater.

The small boat had navigation lights, but she didn't even turn them on. Who would even see them? Maybe aliens.

Ashley's flashlight stood ready to check the status of Whirlpool Alley. But before they even reached the spot, she knew the vortex was running. She could hear it in the night.

Chapter 18

Artificial Intelligence

After the unequivocal success of the night's observations, there was no reason for Tim and Jeremy to stay the additional two days they had planned. Just to be sure they weren't missing anything, they used their test equipment on both telescopes to verify that neither had internal reflections to taint the results. But with Jeremy's scope showing exactly the same fluctuations of the mysterious light as Ashley's smaller telescope, there was really no doubt. The light was real.

So it was best that they got back to work in Arizona. After breakfast (cold cereal, yogurt, and toast), they packed up their equipment and loaded it in the Bayliner. Pissin' down rain had moved in over night, but it couldn't detract from the innate beauty of this place. Jeremy said he wanted to come back in the summer, and Ashley thought he probably would.

They traveled down the lake in fairly good conditions, little more than ripples on the water, punctuated by two-foot chop in some sections. They huddled in the boat's small cabin to stay out of the rain. Two men, a woman, a dog, and lots of baggage. By now it was obvious they all got along well, so it was celebratory but sorrowful goodbyes at the airport.

Tim and Jeremy would go home to report their findings. Then the right people would be thrown into the project, and they'd figure this out. They now knew a light beam was fluctuating mysteriously in (or in front of) Messier 82. What did it mean, and how would they proceed from here? Although that couldn't be answered yet, one thing was sure: they would proceed until they figured it out. If it was related to the swirling whirlpool, that too would be determined. Some of the best astronomers in the world and military on both sides of the border would see to it.

* * * * *

"**W**e're pretty much on overload as far as data is concerned," said Captain Sterling. "The Auroras have downloaded so much stuff that we haven't had time to sort it all out yet. It'll take awhile."

"I haven't seen an airplane for a couple days," replied Ashley.

"That's because we've got more ammunition than we know what to do with. We'll send in a flight now and then, probably a single pass every day. We want to keep track of things, making sure something's still down there."

"Why wouldn't it be?" asked Ashley, but she knew the answer.

"Because it might decide to leave. Or send up another pillar, or something."

"I guess we can count on the 'or something' part."

"Seriously, we won't leave it alone until we figure it out. It's just that right now we're dealing with data we don't understand. I can't give you details, of course, but let's just say its packets of almost indecipherable details. I use the word 'almost' because it shows order, so it's intelligent information. But we can't tell what it's saying."

"Is there any chance it's alive?"

"You know I can't discuss stuff like that. But I'll give you a simple 'No', because we're convinced there's no organic materials involved. We have really sophisticated sniffers."

"Sniffers?"

"Now give me a break, Ashley. You know I've already gone well beyond the bounds I'm allowed. Just trust me – it isn't alive. On the other hand, I've never seen data that's so intelligent. In other words – and this is entirely off the record – it's the highest form of artificial intelligence I've ever seen."

"So there are aliens behind it somewhere."

"Look, Ashley, our Auroras can use their tail stinger to pull all kinds of data out of the lake. That tail extension isn't a secret – it's the MAD boom we usually use to detect submarines. It's also no secret that we use infrared detectors, acoustic equipment, APS-137 radar, and a more sophisticated electronics suite than on the P-3. Maybe someday we'll have some of the new Boeing P-8's the American Navy is buying, but for now the Aurora is top of the line. So, as I said, we're on data overload right now, but we're sorting it out slowly. I promise you'll be given whatever we learn, short of anything that might compromise military secrets. You should consider yourself very privileged."

Sterling was proud of the Aurora, as anyone would expect, but with a typical Canadian hint of indignation for American technology. "Top of the line" sounded almost resentful.

"I do feel privileged, of course. It's a marvelous aircraft. But what's the MAD boom, and that APS thingy?"

"Can't tell you much about the APS-137, except to say it's an inverse synthetic aperture radar. MAD stands for Magnetic Anomaly Detector, used for locating submarines by good-ol'-fashioned magnetism."

"Magnetic Anomaly Detector, eh? Sounds perfect for detecting a lake Anomaly, with a capital 'A'."

"Very funny, Ashley, and a bit coincidental, I must admit. The MAD boom has been used in commercial geologic surveys to detect mineral deposits, too, so we're looking close at that kind of data. Which is way more than I should be telling you. Please, Ashley, don't ask any more questions right now, because I've got to stop talking."

"Okay, I get the message loud and clear: ET, phone home."

* * * * *

Ashley was on the phone these days more than she preferred. Standing at the kitchen counter, tethered to the antenna cord, wasn't exactly comfortable, from either a physical or psychological sense. She hated telephones, which was one of the reasons she lived here – an excuse to stay off the phone. But now she needed the communication. It was an important link to continued involvement with the Anomaly, and that attachment had become strangely compelling.

Jeremy kept her up to date on progress associated with the astronomical aspect of the Anomaly, while Captain Sterling called regularly to brief her regarding Aurora activity. Funny thing – she didn't even know Sterling's first name, yet she never called Jeremy

"Doctor." Both of her contacts were easy-going and fun to work with, but she couldn't figure out why the captain was so concerned with keeping her informed. She could understand Jeremy's openness, since astronomy was a public science. But why the military? One day she decided to ask him.

"Captain, I really appreciate you keeping me updated, but I can't understand why I'm getting VIP treatment."

"Don't argue with success, Ashley. This case hasn't been normal since the very beginning. From our standpoint, we're grateful this hasn't been turned over to a higher authority already. We work for Ottawa, you know. But so far we've been left alone, probably because of the record of the Aurora. We've solved some important things you'll never know about, and that's allowed us to keep the ball in our court."

"Well, I'm happy for you, but I also know you could shut me off, if you wanted to."

"The boss – let's just say he has a lot of stars on his shoulder – has taken a personal interest in this project. He let's me call the shots, while he holds off the powers that be. One of his direct orders to me is to keep you informed of everything… or almost everything."

"The big kahuna."

"You might say that. He wants to keep the Lookie-Loo's out. It's the last thing we need. And we respect your property boundaries."

"Well, there really aren't any boundaries here. I own my cabin, but I lease the water rights from the province."

"Maybe you haven't seen the aerial photo from the Ministry of Agriculture and Lands that designates the boundaries of your lease."

"I've got a document from BC Lands somewhere, but all I know is they charge me five hundred dollars every year for water rights. Water that belongs to all of us. Crown property, you know."

"Well if you look close at the aerial photo, you'll see that your water rights extend out to the whirlpool area."

"I own a flying saucer!" exclaimed Ashley, raising her voice enough to disturb Cassie: *Woof, woof!*

"I heard your dog," quipped the captain.

"She says it belongs to her, too."

"Ashley, let me get serious for a moment. We need your help in keeping people out of there, and that's part of the reason the big kahuna, as you call him, is on your side. We figure you're out there, and we're here in our cushy offices. We don't want any publicity to spoil things. In fact, it could tank the whole thing. We're under a lot of pressure to run everything we find up the flagpole to the powers above us. So far, they've said 'press on,' but that may not work much longer. Already there are science teams pushing to pay you a visit. We're on the opposite fence, asking that they leave things alone for now."

"I wouldn't mind seeing scientists here, trying to sort things out. The team from Arizona wasn't a problem."

"But that's different. They're working on the astronomy side of things. What's under the water is our game, and we're experts at how to play it. I can't give you the details, but there was a similar situation in South America not too long ago."

"Similar to this? Where?"

"No, I can't divulge any more. But I can confide in you that there never was a resolution to what was going on there, because too many people got involved. They didn't have the benefit of Auroras or P-3's. Few people understand, but we can sniff from the air just as well as scientists can sniff from a boat trailing a cable. And it's a lot less intrusive."

"I'm sure you can't tell me, but does that mean the 'situation' in South America is still on-going."

"I'm afraid not. There was a big explosion, not documented in the news, when they left."

* * * * *

Ashley had already worried about that. As much as she wanted this to be resolved, she was concerned that whatever was under the water would simply leave, and they'd never know what it was. When the pillar exploded, she thought it might be gone. The next time there's an explosion, it could be the last.

Captain Sterling reminded her to check the whirlpool area as often as possible, and let him know about any changes she saw — anything at all. He needn't bother, since she was out there in her tin boat every day anyway. Nothing seemed to change. Usually the area was quiet, undisturbed water no different from the rest of the protected area near Third Narrows. When the whirlpool flowed, although there were small variations in how it looked, the vortex was pretty much the same each time. The only thing that made it look different from one occurrence to the next was the extent of flotsam swirling around it. Sometimes it looked more malicious only because more sticks were whirling in its turbulence.

Then one day, after a night when the fluctuating light was again evident in her telescope, she approached Whirlpool Alley in her tin boat with a bit of apprehension. The whirlpool looked normal in scope and extent, even in speed, but it had developed a dull green coloration. You could call it a glow, although it was hard to tell in the sunlight whether it was just a change in the color of the water or an actual luminescence.

That afternoon, after the daily pass of the Aurora, she decided to call Captain Sterling. It was unusual for Ashley to call him, because he contacted her often enough for her to feel it was unnecessary. When he came on the line, she came right to the point.

"Hello, captain. I saw your airplane again today."

"Yes, they're analyzing the data download right now."

"I thought I should notify you about a change in appearance of the whirlpool."

"Sure. Go ahead."

"There's a greenish glow that I've never seen before. It definitely has changed color to a dull green, but bright in the sense that it seems to radiate. If I saw it somewhere else on the lake, I'd probably think someone dropped some oil in the water. In other words, it doesn't look that unusual, at least during daylight."

"So you can't tell whether it's glowing or just a saturation in the water."

"No, but I'll go out after dark, and let you know what I find."

"That would be good, because the lab has already reported that something changed during today's pass. It's a minor aberration from the norm, but it did come up on the initial analysis. While I've got you, there's something I need to tell you."

"That doesn't sound good."

"No, it's not a biggie. But we've lost a minor battle here. You're going to get some visitors."

"You mean besides the ones under the water?"

"Ha, ha. Well, they might be a bit more malicious than that. Scientists from the University of British Columbia. Pretty harmless, probably, but we'd prefer they stayed home."

"It sounds like its time for me to pay you back," said Ashley. "I'll try to keep them under control."

"UBC has signed on the dotted line to avoid any intrusive activity that might disturb the whirlpool – more importantly, what's underneath. But they might get carried away."

"I'll certainly do my best."

"They'll be bringing a Kemmerer bottle, a device for sampling the water. We've approved it, but don't let them drop that bottle directly into the whirlpool. They can take samples as close as 100 feet from the whirlpool, but they're prohibited from dropping right over it. They know the rules, but I don't trust them. So I need your help with this."

"I have a shotgun."

"Really?"

"No, just kidding. But I can whittle a big stick that looks like a shotgun."

* * * * *

Right after dark, Ashley launched the tin boat for the short ride to the whirlpool. But she really didn't need to go – even from the deck of her cabin she could see the glow.

When she arrived at the spot, the water was shimmering with a powerful glow, forest-green. The oval-shaped swirl, lit up like a holiday ornament, extended down far enough that she thought she could see bottom. Squinting and leaning over the side of the boat, she deliberated whether she was viewing something shaped like a submarine.

◊ ◊ ◊ ◊ ◊ ◊ ◊

Chapter 19

Blue Shift

Ashley knew Jeremy would come back to Fortune Lake. She just didn't know it would be this soon.

She met him at the airport, while he was still arguing with an airline agent about his telescope. A forklift was perched at the tail of the Flying Boxcar, but it sat idle, it's metal tongs stopped in the half-raised position.

"It's a fragile telescope. Very expensive. Can't they unload it by hand?"

"They say it's extremely heavy, sir," replied the dark-blue-uniformed woman.

"I loaded it myself in Vancouver. They let me out on the ramp at the South Terminal, and gave me a cargo specialist to assist. The two of us just hoisted it on up into the hold."

"This isn't Vancouver, I'm afraid. We have procedures, you know."

"Procedures. Okay, but can I at least go out there to supervise. I promise not to touch anything."

Just as the agent was about to render her verdict (which didn't look good), Ashley stepped forward.

"Hi, Jane. I see you've already met my friend, Jeremy. Hello, Jeremy! Welcome back."

"Ashley! It's great to see you," said Jeremy, and he obviously meant it. "Can you help with this?"

"What's wrong, Jane?" intervened Ashley. "Can you make an exception for this? It's an expensive telescope, and we're going to use it on Fortune Lake."

"Really? A big telescope on the lake. At your place?"

"Yes, at Third Narrows. Well, it's really not that big, but it's fragile. So could you make an exception this one time? I'll help him get it off the plane."

"Well… okay, but don't tell anybody."

"No, I won't, Jane. Thanks."

The forklift pulled away from the Boxcar, and Jeremy and Ashley slid the metal container out the door and onto a waiting baggage cart. It wasn't very heavy, but it was bulky. The second container accompanying it was heavier, but a lot smaller. Jeremy did most of the lifting, and Ashley just helped guide it onto the cart.

"Some assembly required," quipped Jeremy.

"A replacement for your Schmidt-Cassegrain?"

"Don't I wish? No, it belongs to the university. They purchased it specifically for this project, an apo refractor with an MX mount.

Ashley had heard of apo refractors, but she really didn't know much about them, except they were expensive.

"Not that heavy, is it," said Ashley.

"That's what I tried to tell your friend. We'll have no trouble setting it up."

"I'm just a meek little woman, so the man will have to do all the work."

"Sure," laughed Jeremy, grabbing her healthy looking bicep just below the sleeve of her T-shirt. "You're just a wimp."

They slid the two boxes into the bed of Ashley's truck – no problem. The rest of the equipment and Jeremy's personal bags went into the back seat of the crew cab. Her rear seat was the depository for all-and-everything, and it was seldom completely unloaded. So they struggled a bit to find enough room.

Then they hopped into the front seat of the pickup, although Cassie already occupied Jeremy's side of the seat. The Lab was thrilled to see someone she recognized.

"Good girl! Good girl!" he said, trying to get her to calm down. But Cassie insisted on extending her greeting by circling low on the seat in her typical crazy dance, until finally Jeremy snuck in far enough to close the door. The black Lab was wedged between him and Ashley, a tight fit. Then Cassie settled down with her head on Jeremy's lap, and they were finally on their way to the marina.

Ashley brought the Bayliner around to the launch ramp, where the truck could be backed close enough to the boat for loading. The big box with the telescope was easier to handle this way, since the boat's normal parking spot was a long way from the marina gate.

It was a beautiful day, with spring finally moving into summer. Ashley had removed the canvas cover from the command bridge so they could ride up high, using the duplicate controls with a 360-degree view.

After cruising north for about a half-hour, Ashley angled towards a low island where a self-propelled barge was passing in the opposite direction. She slowed to a stop, and turned off the engine.

"Hello, Fritz!" she yelled from the bridge. "Beauty of a day, eh!"

A small bearded man in bright yellow coveralls and what looked like a plastic bicycle helmet appeared from behind the load: "Hi, Ashley! Now you git back up there to Third Narrows!"

Ashley yelled a laugh towards Fritz, and waved her arm high over her head.

"What are you haulin' today?" she hollered.

"Don't ask!"

She didn't. But she laughed again, and restarted the engine. The Bayliner came back up on-step, and the barge disappeared behind them.

Ashley thought Jeremy would appreciate another stop, this time at one of her favorite spots just before they passed through Third Narrows. When she brought the Bayliner to a halt, glaciated mountains to the north glistened on the water, reflecting their image in the placid lake. It was a reminder of the sublime beauty surrounding this grand lake. And she was right – Jeremy was awestruck.

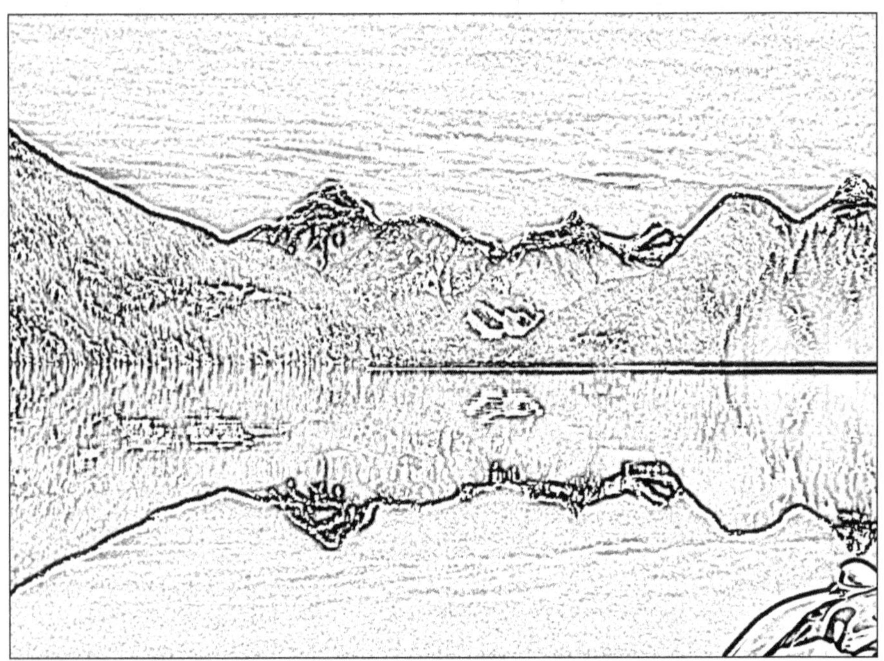

A few minutes later they rounded the point at Third Narrows, the boat riding smoothly on plane. She pulled the throttle back and slowed to a crawl. They motored slowly past the whirlpool, now inactive, and docked at the float cabin.

* * * * *

That evening, Jeremy set up the telescope, while Cassie supervised. It was a hi-tech Quantum 180 on a Paramount MX-5 equatorial wedge. What made this setup remarkable wasn't the telescope, a high-quality apochromatic refractor not much bigger than Ashley's Maksutov-Cassegrain. Instead, it was the precision German mount that got her attention. With this tripod, the 7-inch apo refractor could point and track with an accuracy far beyond Ashley's simpler scope. And it could carry a spectrometer, which was precisely why Jeremy hauled it all the way to Fortune Lake.

While Jeremy set up the hi-tech telescope, Ashley brought her Maksutov out of the kitchen, and placed it in its customary position on the deck. Her small scope might be outperformed tonight, but it wouldn't be forgotten. It had earned the prominent stature of first-discovery, and Ashley was now a surprisingly advanced amateur astronomer.

Justin, if you're watching, what do you think?!

Ashley had the Maksutov-Cassegrain set up well before Jeremy had his cutting-edge equipment running, so she checked on M82. The light was "on" tonight.

Once the apo refractor was focused on the galaxy and the fluctuating light, Jeremy let out a sigh of relief.

"It's a long way from Tucson," he joked.

"So I hear. Now what?"

"Now, my dear friend, we hook up the spectrometer.

* * * * *

After two hours on the deck, taking CCD photos of M82 with Jeremy's laptop hooked up to the MX mount, they exchanged the camera for the compact spectrometer. After that, Ashley was pretty much lost, but Jeremy explained things when they were back inside the cabin, warming themselves over cups of hot cocoa.

Ashley pulled off her maroon sneakers, and slipped on furry slippers with giant rabbit ears sticking out. When she spoke, it was with more astronomical authority than she realized she possessed.

"I've heard apochromatic refractors use internal light baffles. Does that really help?"

"This one has four baffles, and that's part of the reason we selected it for this project. A fluctuating light in this baby is almost certainly a fluctuating light. But the big deal is the MX mount. It's so damn precise during tracking, and the software is amazing. Did you know Joseph Fraunhofer proposed the design, minus the computer, two hundred years ago?"

"I've heard of him. Famous instrument maker."

"Very famous, to say the least. But we're both going to be famous when they see the spectrometer results."

"Which tells us what?"

"Well, we'll need to wait for the lab in Arizona to run all of the data. I'll send it to them as soon as we get back to town. But the main thing is what's most obvious, although preliminary, of course – there's a blue shift."

"You're kidding! It's headed towards us?"

"That's what a blue shift means, but that doesn't apply to M82. It's receding at 200 kilometers per second. We've known that for a long time. The fluctuating object is where we're picking up the blue shift."

"So M82 sits far behind the Anomaly."

"A long ways. Maybe your Anomaly is not so far away, after all. We'll need to see what the lab says, but it could be almost any distance. Who knows?"

"They know," kidded Ashley, gesturing towards the whirlpool.

"Probably they do, and that partly explains the coincidence of the events. If the Anomaly were associated with M82, then it would be 12 million light-years away and have to be extraordinarily bright to be seen in your telescope. But if it's a lot closer, then it could be a lot dimmer and still be visible."

"And then it could send communication signals to the whirlpool in real time."

"That's still a bit of a stretch," said Jeremy. "It's probably at least a few light-years away, so we still have the problem of time lag. Unless, as we sometimes say, 'Einstein is dead',"

"Or unless it's sitting out there no farther than Mars."

"Well, I suppose. We really need to wait for the lab to decide. But here's the ultra-cool thing. We sit here on Fortune Lake, a long way from anywhere, and no one else can see this fluctuating light. To see it, you actually need to be here with you own little telescope."

"Yes, that's way cool," replied Ashley. "But I haven't noticed you mentioning the collimated light problem. It still makes it hard to understand how we might see an object that can't be seen in an 8-meter telescope in Hawaii."

"It's still a major dilemma, but less so now that we know the object is closer to earth. Besides, there's still much to learn about what makes light act the way it does. We probably know a lot less than those little green men."

"I bet they're women."

Chapter 20

Big Kahuna

Jeremy stayed an extra day, though it wasn't necessary. He had all the data he needed, but he wanted to transmit it to Tucson right away. So they went to town the next morning, and took care of the extensive email attachments in the lobby of the hotel. Then they drove back to the marina, and spent the day exploring the lake. They anchored near the island where they'd seen Fritz, fished for trout, and celebrated with wine coolers, while Cassie snacked on strips of beef jerky. Jeremy was enthralled by Fortune Lake, and she knew he would return many times, and soon. But first he needed to enjoy his 15 minutes of fame in Arizona.

Just before sunset, Ashley pulled back into the marina to drop Jeremy off. He'd stay at the hotel in town, and take the first flight out in the morning.

"It's been fun," he said.

"More fun than I've had in a very long time. I hope you come back this summer."

"I'll be here. You can count on it."

"Is there anything else I need to do regarding the near-by source of light? You'll notice I'm emphasizing the words 'near-by'."

"I hope it is close to us. We'll know soon. In the meantime, there's nothing for you to do. I'll report our findings to the IAU, although the original discovery will be credited to you. Harvard still has your report on file from last year."

"You mean when they ignored Justin."

"They really had no choice. If it couldn't be seen with an 8-meter telescope, it obviously didn't exist."

"So do I get to name it?"

"As a matter of fact, you do. Have you been thinking about what you'll call it?"

"How about Cassie?"

* * * * *

When Ashley answered the phone the next morning, the voice was raspy and new.

"Hello, Ashley. This is the big kahuna."

"Oh, how are you sir?"

"I'm fine. Just fine. I thought I should call, based on what Captain Sterling just delivered to my office. Sorry, my name is Clifford Franks."

"And I bet you have a military rank that I should use."

"I do, but just call me 'Cliff.' I feel like I already know you."

For a fleeting moment, that sounded a bit creepy. With Auroras overhead every day, what could they see inside her cabin? How many watts for her solar panel inverter? What radio station was she's listening to? Were Cassie and Ashley rolling around on the rug?

"Captain Sterling tells me you have a hard time keeping the wolves at bay," said Ashley.

"You could say that," laughed the raspy voice. "I just wanted to call to let you know we're all grateful for how you're handling this situation, and to personally bring you up to date on a few things."

"Okay, I appreciate it. I suppose you heard about my report on the whirlpool conditions – the glow and all."

"In fact, that was very useful information. On our next sweep after your report we tried a few different gadgets, and came up with some interesting results."

"You call them 'gadgets'?"

"I don't, but you might. Or you could call them gizmos, if you prefer."

Cliff was another fun guy. Maybe the whole concept of fun is in the eye of the beholder. Like buying something new that you've never seen before, and then noticing they are everywhere on the streets. Maybe fun can be just like that.

"So what do your gadgets tell you?"

"When we tweaked them after hearing about the luminescence, we began receiving rough alphanumerics approximating text. A form of communication. We've just gotten started, but already it looks promising."

"So are they speaking English?"

"Not by a long shot. They actually speak French – Sorry, that was a bad attempt at a Canadian joke."

"It's funny to me!"

"We need you to keep us posted on anything you detect regarding changes in the whirlpool – the color, changes of rotational speed, anything that seems to be different. Maybe you can set up a schedule to go out there every few hours, if it wouldn't be too much trouble. Night observations are particularly valuable, because your reports regarding the emission of colored light have been very helpful. I'll tell you right now that we think there's a relationship between the light and other activity under the water. The color may be crucial."

"Okay, I'll do that. Actually, I'll use anything for an excuse to go out in my tin boat."

"You've got one of those? Aren't they great? I have one at my cottage in Shuswap. There's nothing like bombing around in a tin boat."

Now, really, how can you not like this guy? Aliens are invading, and we're talking about tin boats.

"My sentiments, exactly. Shall I report what I find to you or Captain Sterling?"

"You'll find it's easiest to get through to Sterling. I'm the big kahuna, you know, so I've got to keep circling the wagons."

"Of course," she laughed. "And he'll arrange to pay for my gas?"

"Oh, I didn't think of that. We probably have a small budget somewhere we can use for gas, though it's not something we normally…"

"I was just kidding," she interrupted.

"I should have known. By the way, you should be seeing those UBC folks in the next few hours. I understand they're already in Blue Ridge, and have chartered a boat."

"I'll be careful with them."

"Yes, I hear you have a shotgun."

* * * * *

Auroras were passing overhead more regularly now, often returning for additional low passes just before sunset, even sometimes after dark.

Ashley never failed to wave, and the flight crew never failed to rock their wings when they pulled up and departed for home.

The UBC scientists arrived the morning after she talked to the big kahuna, and they were no problem at all. They must have received the word, for they stayed well away from Whirlpool Alley, dropping their Kemmerer bottle five times, all well away from the vortex. They stopped in briefly to check with Ashley, and she offered them pop: "No, thanks," one of them said. "We're on our way back to Blue Ridge. Mission accomplished."

She never heard anything about them again. By now Ashley had come to realize the data being collected by the Aurora was as good as it gets. Probably the UBC study would allow some postdocs to get fellowship credit. No more, no less.

* * * * *

The spectrometric analysis from the lab in Tucson was fairly straightforward. The biggest news was that the object was definitely not in M82, but well in front of it. When Jeremy reported the results to her, he added a few facts about the situation in Arizona she didn't expect.

"I should tell you we have a complete clamp-down on this whole thing for now. I'm sure it's only temporary, and it has nothing to do with freedom of speech, so please don't misunderstand."

"In other words, everybody has to keep their mouths shut, but it's for the country's good. I've heard that one before, but fortunately never in the States. Until now."

"The real problem, according to our government hush-your-mouth sources, is the other part of the Anomaly, your whirlpool. Until that's resolved, we really shouldn't announce anything about the astronomical findings. If the military loses control of the whirlpool data, we could be in trouble. So it needs to be resolved before you become famous."

"Actually, I think I follow your reasoning. We don't want an influx of people in Third Narrows, and releasing your findings could cause that to happen."

"Wouldn't you just love it if Third Narrows was suddenly on the map, big time?"

"You know I wouldn't. And you're right, it could damage the project involving the whirlpool."

"That's why we're trying to keep a lid on things here," explained Jeremy. "Once the whirlpool mystery is solved, we should be able to get everything out in the open."

The Canadian military, working in conjunction with their American counterparts, had somehow managed to keep Jeremy's part of the project under wraps, which made some sense. But Ashley figured they couldn't maintain control of a thing like this for long. Jeremy thought the astronomical data would be announced soon. How soon, he couldn't say.

"So Washington is where your pressure is coming from, not the military?" suggested Ashley.

"We're a lot closer to Washington, figuratively speaking, and we don't operate in isolation here at the university," concluded Jeremy. "Wish we did."

"Well, I'm surprised the Canadian military has been able to keep things out of the hands of their government, at least for now. As we always say on the lake: 'We're a long way from Ottawa.'"

"These days, nobody's very far from anybody else," noted Jeremy. "Getting back to the fluctuating light. Your object isn't inside M82, but a long ways in front of it instead."

"So the galaxy hasn't anything to do with the object," Ashley said, testing the waters. "The fluctuating light just happens to be located between M82 and earth."

"Right, it's not in M82, but I have a theory about that. The light might not be in the galaxy, but it could have come from it."

"Oh. You mean the object was sent out from there, and it's been on its way towards earth for a very long time – really big numbers with lots of zeros."

"Dare I use the word 'mothership'?" asked Jeremy.

"And your lab is sure the spectrum has a blue shift?" she asked.

"It's conclusive. Not very far on the blue side, so it's barely moving, but definitely headed towards us. We won't have a distance estimate for a few more days, because we'll need a parallax shift from observatories on opposite sides of the earth. Chile and Australia are working on it now."

"But how can they get a parallax shift, if they can't see it. I thought only us Fortune Lake people were blessed with that."

"Well, there's some major egg on faces around here. It turns out you can't see it except from your house, but that's only true of the visible light. Don't forget there's a whole lot of spectrum on both sides."

"Oh," replied Ashley, pausing briefly to let her brain catch up with her mouth. Jeremy must have known she was pondering things, because he waited for her to continue.

"I think I get it," said Ashley. "So all of a sudden, everybody can see this thing, as long as they're not using one of those old fashioned optical telescopes."

"Well, not everybody, but there's a strong signal in the microwave band."

"That raises a whole bunch of questions in this struggling little brain of mine. Like, does it mean there's a pulsing signal coming out of this thing in only the optical range, and everybody else – microwave, for example – sees a steady light in their part of the spectrum?"

"No, it's flickering for everybody, but only the visual band is intensely collimated. A high-beam focused laser at one place in the spectrum, and a low-beam flashlight elsewhere. Now, why it wouldn't be visible as a distant pencil of visible light from other locations beats me, but it could be technology that's so advanced we may as well consider it magic."

"Okay, I think I get it. But why would little green women do this?"

"I've got a theory there, too."

"That figures."

"Well, suppose it's a signal used to communicate with your little submarine without raising a lot of attention. They send out a pulsing signal that can only be seen at Third Narrows, and they cut down dramatically on their chance of detection."

"And they elect to do this in the visible spectrum."

"You're right. It doesn't make sense why they wouldn't use microwave or X-ray. Anything can pack more information than visible light. And think of the power needed to keep that thing going."

"Which raises the question of whether it's two-way communication," said Ashley. "Is there any way to tell if the spaceship is receiving messages from our friends in Fortune Lake?"

"Not for us astronomers. But if you owned a sub chaser, you could tell whether they're transmitting. Oh, wait, you do own an Aurora."

"Pretty much. So what else am I missing here, mister astronomer?"

"Well, first, we've never come across light as collimated as this. And, on a different front, we won't be able to estimate size and absolute magnitude until we have a distance estimate. But here's the hot part…"

"How hot?"

"Maybe extremely hot. The spectrogram shows a strong hydrogen emission line, which is normal for a star. But some of the lines seem to have high atomic numbers, which aren't abundant in nature. One unexpected line looks like molybdenum or a similar metal."

"So it's a star, and it's not a star. How do you deal with data like that?"

"We have our ways, Fraulein," quipped Jeremy. "Actually, it's pretty tricky, but I've come up with an idea."

"Let me make a wild guess – it's a spaceship."

"Could be. We'll still need a distance estimate to tie all of this stuff together. But a huge fusion-powered engine, tossing out a signature like a miniature star, might cause a spectrum like this. That would account for the spectrum lines for hydrogen and maybe the other metals as well.

"But wouldn't a strong burst of hydrogen big enough to be seen on a spectrogram mean the fusion exhaust is pointed right at us."

"Right again, Fraulein. In my cockamamie theory, this spaceship is headed right for us, giant retrorockets blazing, and slowing down."

"Whoa, Nelly!" mocked Ashley.

Chapter 21

Data Download

Summer had arrived at Third Narrows. This was the most beautiful time of the year on the lake, were it not for all the people. Of course, only a small portion of the boats on Fortune Lake made it this far north, except for the routine transit of logging crews. But in the summer, pleasure craft often poked their way into Ashley's bay. If they ventured this far in the warm sun, they wanted the complete tour. "Lookie-Loo!" Ashley would exclaim. *Woof, woof!* repeated Cassie.

Once in a while, a boat would come close enough to see the whirlpool, but it wasn't an obvious landmark, even when it was running, so most went right on past without stopping. Even the unusual colors in the water (now a mild yellow) didn't stand out during the day. And no one came near Whirlpool Alley at night, except Ashley in her tin boat and an occasional Lockheed CP-140 Aurora.

Fun had returned to Third Narrows, and Ashley took full advantage of it. During the day, she bombed around in her tin boat, rode her quad into the backcountry, and worked in her garden. John still arrived promptly on Mondays and Thursdays, and she looked forward to each visit.

One day, after John split some wood and helped Ashley water the planters and her upper garden of potatoes on the cliff, they sat at the picnic table drinking root beer. John's ears perked up when he heard an airplane approaching from the north, but neither he nor Ashley stood up until an Aurora suddenly blasted over the cliff.

"Holy shit!" he yelled, jumping to his feet.

Woof, woof! Cassie barked enthusiastically.

John watched the aircraft pass over his own cabin across the bay and then pull up and rock its wings. As he turned back to Ashley, now standing beside Cassie, he scrunched his neck and raised his eyebrows in a questioning way.

"What's that all about?" he asked.

"They come over every once in a while," she replied calmly. "Practicing down low."

"Gonna' smash into somethin', if they're not careful," said John, much less flustered now.

He turned back to the south, his hand over his eyes, trying to see the disappearing airplane in the afternoon sun. But he didn't asked anything more, because that's the way he was. She loved him for it.

"Guess it's time to get home for supper," he said.

She stood a few feet in front of him, purple *UW* baseball cap tilted down to keep the sun away, pony tail sticking out from behind. Her plain tan T-shirt and dark blue shorts, coupled with the hat, gave her an athletic look. She was a woman of the lake, maestro of Third Narrows. An off-the-grid warrior in a daily battle with nature – a skirmish she enjoyed and almost always won.

"Thanks for everything," she replied, which were always her words when she sent him on his way.

"No problem." Which was always his stock reply.

"You're okay with everything?" he added unexpectedly. "Nothin' botherin' you, is there?"

"No, everything's fine. Why do you ask?"

"Well you seem different lately. Don't know why, just different."

"Maybe it's because I'm happy again."

John paused and thought about it: "That's probably it then."

He stood up and stepped down to the lower deck, headed towards the long-fingered dock where his boat was parked. Cassie followed him, so he stopped first to scratch her neck: "Good girl!" he said, and Cassie raised her head to accept the attention.

Then he stepped aboard the Campion, parked first in the line of boats. He pulled the hinged engine cover up to reveal the small but powerful Volvo engine, pulled out the dipstick, and checked the oil.

Then he closed the hinged lid, hopped back onto the lower deck, and walked slowly but purposefully to the Bayliner, next in line. Once again, he stepped aboard, pulled open the engine compartment, and checked the oil. Then he was back on the float, headed towards his own boat.

"Lookin' good!" he yelled back over his shoulder. "You be good now."

Ashley nodded, a big smile on her still-girlish pretty face.

After John started his outboard engine and waited a minute for it to fully warm up, he motored away slowly, towards his rental cabin across the bay. He passed near the whirlpool, but Ashley couldn't see if he looked at it. John seldom missed things this obvious, but often he chose not to mention them, which was a good thing in this case.

In a few minutes, Ashley heard John's chainsaw start up. It ran for about ten minutes, then stopped, and there was a pause for a few minutes. Then the echo of his hammer swept across the bay for a few strong-arm strokes of fixing whatever it was that needed fixing.

Another silence, followed by an outboard motor starting, and the Hourston pulled away towards the Narrows. John waved, and Ashley waved back, smiling broadly from her deck. The Hourston came slowly up on plane, and John sat focused straight ahead, never looking back.

* * * * *

While the astronomers sought a distance measurement for the fluctuating light, the military continued to extract information from the depths of Fortune Lake. Ashley watched the Auroras continue to fly by each day, and occasionally heard them roar overhead in the middle of the night. Every few hours during the day and at least once each night, she slipped away from the cabin in her tin boat to check the whirlpool.

"The vortex is bigger now, at least a bit," said Ashley to Captain Sterling over the phone. "I don't have any way to really measure it, except to line it up against the side of my boat. But it's definitely bigger, about 18 feet in length, and more oval than before."

"The color is still yellow?" asked Sterling.

"Yes, a dull yellow, almost orange, but a brighter tone now. I don't know how to describe it except to say it seems more brilliant in the daytime and glows more at night. A slight shift in color the last few days, from green to yellow, and now almost orange. I told Cliff I'd report any changes, no matter how minor."

"You called him 'Cliff'?"

"Yes."

"Oh." After a pregnant pause, Captain Sterling, cleared his throat and continued.

"I should tell you that the last pass of our CP-140 was amazing. Data popping out all over, and it gets more structured all the time. 'Cliff' thinks it's developing a rudimentary language of some sort. Far from anything we can understand, but with more structure every day."

"Amazing. You get all that by simply eavesdropping as you pass over?"

"Well, you know I can't comment. But I can tell you our pings are getting plenty of replies."

"Pings? So you aren't only receiving data, you're sending it. Sounds like communication to me."

"The object, or whatever it is, is reacting to every electromagnetic pulse we send out. It's two-way in that sense."

"But you can't see what it looks like."

"No comment."

"Oh, com'on, I know it's just your way of saying 'Yes'." She scrunched her lips in her childish pouty pose, wishing he could see.

"It's not a 'Yes.' We have some amazing equipment that gives us visual images underwater and feedback in a variety of frequencies. But that's common knowledge, not even secret. Infrared and radar, for example – ancient technology."

"But you still can't see what it looks like."

"Stop it, Ashley! We could see what it looks like, if there was anything there! But here's the weird part – there isn't."

* * * * *

"**S**till no estimate of the distance," said Jeremy. "Not enough parallax yet, which tends to tell me it's farther away than I expected."

"And what did you expect?"

"Well not so far away that we can't detect a parallax shift on a baseline between Chile and Australia."

"So what do you do now? Send them a telegram?"

"We wait. In another few months the earth will move far enough in its orbit to get a parallax value, unless it's even too far away for that."

"So what's your best guess, based on what you do know?"

"If I add what I know to what I imagine, I come up with less than a light year. But bear in mind the lack of any parallax makes it less and less likely all the time."

"I'd like to know how your imagination calculated that, Jeremy, but I doubt I'd understand."

"You would. Because if it's a spacecraft, it can be only so large, at least according to some back-of-the-envelope calculations they've made around here. And the fusion drive has a theoretical heat limit, too, if you consider metals we know about. So here's how it goes – spacecraft only so big, flame only so hot, distance only so far. You couldn't even see it more than a few light-years away. In fact, that's using very liberal figures. I think it's a lot closer."

"But we won't know for months."

"Six months would give us the greatest spread in parallax from the earth's orbit, so I sure hope it's before then."

"Man, this is giving me a headache," said Ashley. "And I thought we were having too much fun for aches and pains. It's a galaxy. It's a star. It's a spacecraft."

"I go for the spacecraft," replied Jeremy.

"Okay, that's it then – Cassie, the spacecraft."

* * * * *

That night, when Ashley boarded her tin boat with Cassie and cranked up the outboard motor, rain was beginning to fall – small drops sprinkling down on the calm water. She pushed away from the parking spot with a quick thrust of her hand against the dock, and then motored out of the breakwater and over to the whirlpool. It was always running these days, the color now completely transitioned from yellow to orange. Whirlpool Alley was brighter and bigger, growing all the time now.

Approaching the spot, Ashley turned off the motor, as she usually did, drifting closer and hearing only the swirl of the water and the faint popping sound of the rain, as bigger drops now fell around her. She felt peaceful, as if the life below her was trying to communicate by putting her at ease. It was working. Day or night, no matter what the season, Fortune Lake was the most peaceful place on earth. Maybe that's why this spot had been chosen for this.

In the distance, she heard the Aurora growing louder as it approached. She'd never been near the whirlpool during a low pass, and now she had the opportunity. There was no question of safety. The big airplane would pass low overhead, and she might even hear the wingtip vortices swirl, as sometimes occurred in calm conditions.

Closer and closer, she could hear the power coming off the throaty engines as the pilot maneuvered lower and then leveled out, setting up for the low pass. The cliff to the north blocked her view, but she knew the airplane was coming. Closer and closer.

Suddenly it broke into view over the rock wall, its massive frame covering the cliff and her cabin. It continued straight over the whirlpool and her tin boat, and then out over John's cabin to the south. The wingtip vortices sang with a prolonged *Whoosh!*

Woof, woof! yipped Cassie.

And then it drew quiet, except for the swirling of the whirlpool, the background sound of the rain hitting the water, and the diminishing sound of the turboprops. As the pilot pulled up for his traditional rock of the wings, she could see his red and green nav lights alternately bounce up, then down, then up. Out of the corner of her eye, she thought she saw the light of the whirlpool blink twice, and then it was steady again. Faintly, in the background, she heard a high-pitched clicking sound that seemed to join the sound of the rain, momentarily pouring down on Whirlpool Alley. They were in perfect synchronization for a few seconds, like primitive music, and then the clicking sound was gone.

* * * * *

"That's quite a report," said Captain Sterling. "No wonder we pay you those big bucks."

"You pay me enough by letting me stay in my home. I have the feeling I could have done a lot worse."

"We've been getting lots of audio from the Aurora downloads, too. Especially the last few days. Something's changing, but none of our experts can put their finger on it. Your Anomaly is showing increased signs of intelligence, or maybe it's developing a language we'll eventually understand. When we pinged it last night, it replied with rough textual bursts. At least that's what we think was happening."

"You're talking scary now," replied Ashley.

"I don't want to scare you, but I need to get through to you on something. Some of our engineering consultants see indications this thing is going to blow. If it was just one engineer or just one reason, I'd say forget it. But there's a lot of uncorrelated data pointing in the same direction."

"That's no surprise. I feel it, too. Of course, I'm not an engineer."

"Which provides another important data point to consider," said Captain Sterling. "Do you really feel it?"

Ashley thought about that for a few moments, and when Sterling didn't speak right away, she took even a few more seconds to organize her thoughts. When she spoke, it was in a tone that registered a level of seriousness coupled with a timidity that suggested she didn't expect to be believed.

"You know, Captain, there has been some weirdness lately that I haven't told you about, but only because it's so silly. You wanna' hear?"

"Of course. You'd be amazed at the level of weirdness we see in this data from our cushy offices. I can only imagine what it's like from your front porch."

"It's not from the porch that I feel it so much, although sometimes I get strange vibes when I'm aboard the float. Mostly just a feeling that somebody is trying to talk to me, but nothing specific coming through. When it gets intense is when I'm in my tin boat, checking on Whirlpool Alley. When I get close, everything seems to slow down, and I lose track of where I am. It's very peaceful, actually. I don't hear anything, but I feel the presence of whatever is down there. And I find myself gradually becoming more convinced those little green women are getting ready to leave, and that makes me sad."

Captain Sterling paused, and then spoke in his matter-of-fact voice: "They're talking to you. And they're talking to us, too, but in a much more formal way."

"Well, I must admit it seems like they're trying to talk, but there's been so much going on…"

"I'm not surprised," remarked Captain Sterling. "We've interpreted our data pretty much the same way. But if they're leaving, the big question is why?"

"Well, my gut feeling says they're done. As simple as that. Maybe they didn't come to stay, but only to gather whatever information they're looking for, and now they're done. It's a lab, of sorts, not unlike your fancy Auroras, but they've come from a bit farther away."

"A few light years, I suppose," commented the captain. "And what about the other half of your anomaly up there among the constellations?"

"For that I have nothing but a wild guess. You'd have to ask those geeks in Arizona. But my preference is to think of that fluctuating light as the mothership. More little green women waiting in the wings."

"Now that would be cool!" said Sterling, with a lift in his voice. "Maybe they ain't gonna' blow us out of the sky, after all."

"Well, don't worry about me. I'm prepared to keep out of the way," replied Ashley.

"Ladies and gentlemen, stand back away from your TV sets," kidded the captain.

"I would if I had a TV set."

"We don't want to disturb it, but it's taking the initiative," said Captain Sterling. "The Aurora data streams seem to detect feedback loops even before we ping. It's as if it hears us coming."

"I'm sure it does hear you coming. I can hear the airplane from a long way out."

"No, I don't mean audible sound. I'm talking about electromagnetic pulses that are normally line-of-sight. While we're still behind the mountain, setting up for the pass, it starts pinging us. We're not sure how."

"Mind readers," replied Ashley.

"More to the point, we think it's reacting in established ways now, more like a person than a machine."

"It's talking to you, too," said Ashley.

Woof, woof!

"That's your dog again, isn't it?"

"She gets excited when I get excited."

"You see what I mean?" said Captain Sterling.

Chapter 22

Stellar Pillar

After the night when the whirlpool blinked and sang with the rain, Ashley never returned to the area of the vortex. It wasn't a matter of fear, although it was related to self-protection. The whirlpool never threatened her. Even the explosion and the towering pillar hadn't seemed malicious. She had an unwritten contract with this lake that said she could stay as long as she wanted. Her end of the deal required that she respect the lake in return. In her mind, the contract was forever.

But it didn't mean she would stand idly by while the whirlpool wound itself up and spun out of control. It never seemed poised to do that, at least not on the surface of the water. But no one knew what was underneath. Self-assurance was a trait she understood, for she had it, then lost it, and then found it again. She didn't know exactly how she knew the vortex was about to blow, but she knew. She knew it was reaching back towards the stars, and that was where it should go.

During all of her years on the float, with and without Justin, she'd always talked to herself. Crazy people did things like that, as well as those who wanted to avoid going crazy. Besides, how different was it from talking to your dog?

"Cassie, that thing's going to blow!"

Woof, woof, woof!

"It's time to go, girl. We need to be out in the boat where we're safe, rather than waiting here, much too close."

No *Woof,* but a wag of the tail.

"We need to be a bit careful. Because we're going to be here a long, long time."

Woof, woof!

"It's time, Cassie. But I haven't the slightest idea how I know."

She knew it was time, but didn't feel there was any hurry. Somehow, she felt the whirlpool was waiting for her to start the clock.

Thus, in a relative relaxed mood, considering the situation, Ashley washed the few dishes sitting in the sink, so her home would be clean when she returned. Then she sat down on the yellow-flowered couch and opened her laptop computer.

"Being practical to the end, I really should make a backup copy of my new e-book," she said to Cassie, who sat staring at her. "Ever heard of electromagnetic pulse? It's deadly on hard drives."

The dog stirred, licked her chops, and plopped down on the rug in front of the wood stove.

It only took a few keystrokes to backup the e-book file to a USB memory stick. Just in case, she copied her banking folder the same way. Then Ashley slipped the memory stick into the pocket of her jeans. As she was about to turn off the laptop, it beeped at her, and a message popped up in a blue box: *File waiting – download now?*

Which would have been okay, if she was connected to the Internet. Which she wasn't.

When Ashley clicked the download icon, a brief textual message popped up, surrounded by a blue box outline.

Thanks for help. Beautiful place.

Learned from you. Back again later.

"Cassie, I guess it's safe to say you didn't send this."

Woof, woof!

* * * * *

Out in Third Narrows, far enough on the far side of the main channel to feel comfortable, Ashley positioned the Bayliner so it could drift engine-off a long way without reaching shore. From here, she had a good view of her home and the place where the whirlpool spun in its orange light. It was too deep to anchor here, but she would be safe with Cassie, as long as the explosion was no bigger than the first.

She needed to give Cassie an ass-push to get the big Lab up the steps to the command bridge. From up here, the summer sun beat down on them with welcome intensity, but not so hot as to be uncomfortable in the light breeze coming through the Narrows. It was almost always this way on a clear summer day – an up-lake wind developing slowly as the day goes by. Like everything else about this lake, she felt at home with a wind that provided few surprises to spoil her day.

After a few minutes, drifting and snacking on trail mix, Ashley made sure Cassie still had plenty of her favorite dog-bits in her Bayliner bowl on the upper helm. It looked like the dog hadn't eaten a morsel, so she shook the bowl, but Cassie ignored it.

The air became suddenly still, the up-lake breeze gone in an instant. A feeling of heavy moisture might have been what made Cassie bark in a clipped tone: *Woof!*

Ashley stared at her home, where it sat drenched in sunlight. Suddenly, an immense flash caused her to reflexively turn her head and close her eyes. She held them closed while grabbing Cassie's neck, pushing her head down. The dog didn't struggle, as if she knew she was being protected.

The massive explosion was quickly followed by a magical quiet that swept over the Bayliner on the coattails of a warm wind from the west. The gentle breeze suddenly soothed her, and caused her to open her eyes and let go of Cassie's head.

"It's okay, girl. Everything is okay."

Woof!

As if she understood, one *woof* was enough.

Now Ashley turned back to the source of the brilliant light, where the small whirlpool had been. The loud rushing noise she'd heard once before was all around her, and an amber pillar rose from the water between the Bayliner and John's floating cabin. It gushed upward, narrow and polished on the sides, rising towards the sky. The clouds today were puffy cumulus, scattered from horizon to horizon, and the pillar pushed right through the middle of one, and kept on going.

Then the shock wave arrived, a resounding boom followed by a tidal-like surge of water that rocked the Bayliner, but it didn't even register a *woof* from Cassie.

Woman and dog sat there, almost motionless, for at least a minute, watching the pillar rise towards the heavens. Ashley was smiling now, a mix of happiness and regret. Then came the low-pitched howl she remembered from before. The rain was coming, and it would be in big drops that would obscure her view in all directions.

Rain poured down, drenching her and Cassie.

"It's okay. It's okay," she repeated, but Cassie didn't bark.

When the rain finally stopped, after about five minutes, the pillar was gone. So Ashley squared her small frame in the captain's chair, pulled her baseball cap down over her forehead, and started the engine.

"Cassie, what do you say we go home?"

Woof, woof!

Chapter 23

Floating on a Lake

When she got back to the cabin, all was exactly as she'd left it, and her kitchen dishes were clean. John's cabin across the bay looked unchanged, but she'd check it more closely tomorrow. When he came by to help her on Thursday, it would be nice to let him know his property had been looked after with the attention it deserved. Maybe John would have heard about the star named "Cassie" by then, if it still existed. But he'd probably not pay it any mind.

The phone rang several times that afternoon, until she finally turned it off. Captain Sterling and Jeremy would be trying to reach her, but they knew she could take care of herself. So the phone could wait.

The whirlpool was gone, so there was no need to check on it. Yet, the tin boat needed a mission, so she'd go over to Sandy Beach with Cassie later that day, and hunt for driftwood small enough to burn in the stove when winter came. When you live in a float cabin, it's best to be prepared.

Tonight, she'd carry the Maksutov-Cassegrain out onto the deck, and look at M82. It would be floating high above the cliff, riding in front of the Big Dipper, which traveled upside-down this time of year. She'd align her telescope, probably using Arcturus and another bright star. Arcturus was one of her favorites, ever since Justin had taught her how easy it was to find: "Arc to Arcturus," he'd always say.

But when she focused on M82, she didn't expect to find a fluctuating light, for it would probably be gone. If it was still there, she would call it "Cassie," and watch it one last time, because she expected the twinkling light to be receding fast.

This was a time for something new and bright, and the summer stars were rising, brilliant Vega leading the parade. Maybe she'd try

Andromeda, Messier 31, if she could stay awake until midnight. It would rise in the east, drooped below Cassiopeia, the W-shaped constellation that reminded her of a dog.

Like any serious amateur astronomer, she spread out her sky chart in the bright of day, sliding it around on the couch with the muted yellow flowers to see the stars from different angles. She'd be prepared for tonight, unless she changed her mind and went to bed early. Which she deserved.

When she went to sleep, no matter what time it was, she'd leave the patio door unlocked, as she always did, for there was no inside lock. Who would she be trying to keep out, anyway?

Tomorrow, Ashley would go to town with Cassie, if the winds and waves cooperated. If not, they had enough food to last a light-year, maybe more. As long as Cassie's beef jerky held out, there was no hurry.

As these indeterminate plans passed comfortably through her mind, she heard a sound in the distance, the dull roar of Allison engines that always drew her out onto the deck. So she stepped outside.

Cassie stood beside her, under a sky still speckled with puffy cumulus clouds, cloaking a bright sheet of blue. The mournful cry of a loon, somewhere in John's back bay, called to its mate, or maybe it was disturbed by the sound of the approaching Aurora.

Ashley could feel the float moving, ever so gently in the light breeze. The motion of her home was subdued, as was usually the case, always in the background. The gentle movement somehow affected everything about her, a subtle influence on how she thought and how she functioned.

She saw the CP-140 Aurora maneuvering to the east, dropping down behind the mountains to begin its turn to the north, and then its low pass. Cassie sat up at attention, waiting for what they both knew was coming.

When the big airframe surged over the cliff with the tremendous roar she'd heard so many times before, she waved and shouted. "It's okay now! It's okay!"

Woof, woof, woof!

The big airplane flew straight and level, not deviating a bit from its path until well past John's cabin. But this time it didn't rock it's wings as it climbed out of sight. Instead, it stayed lower to the ground than usual, and swung around in a bank to the left, a tight but graceful turn. Now it was facing her head-on, descending even more, and closing fast.

For once she could see it approaching her home, because the cliff wasn't in the way. The Aurora blasted straight towards her, even lower than the previous pass, flying directly over Whirlpool Alley, and then straight toward her cabin. And as it approached, so close and so low, it rocked its wings in big graceful arcs, a final salute goodbye. Then it rushed past the cliff to the north, and was gone.

About the Author

From 1980 to 2005, Wayne Lutz was Chairman of the Aeronautics Department at Mount San Antonio College in Los Angeles. He also served 20 years as a U.S. Air Force C-130 aircraft maintenance officer. His educational background includes a B.S. degree in physics from the University of Buffalo and an M.S. in systems management from the University of Southern California. The author is a flight instructor with 7000 hours of flying experience.

For the past three decades, he has spent summers in Canada, exploring remote regions in his Piper Arrow, camping next to his airplane. The author resides in a floating cabin on Canada's Powell Lake in all seasons, and occasionally in a city-folk condo in Bellingham, Washington. His writing genres include regional Canadian publications and science fiction.

Coastal British Columbia Stories

by Wayne J. Lutz

Up the Lake
Up the Main
Up the Winter Trail
Up the Strait
Up the Airway
Farther Up the Lake
Farther Up the Main
Farther Up the Strait
Cabin Number 5
Off the Grid
Up the Inlet
Beyond the Main
Powell Lake by Barge and Quad

Future Titles:
Islands and Inlets
Beneath the Waters of Coastal BC

Order at:
www.PowellRiverBooks.com

* * * * *

Coastal BC Living Blog
PowellRiverBooks.blogspot.com

www.ingramcontent.com/pod-product-compliance
Lightning Source LLC
Chambersburg PA
CBHW071813190726
48292CB00008B/2816